"Why Do You Keep Showing Up Like This?"

Lynda asked Kent as he settled himself behind the steering wheel.

"Why?" The smile that had been on his face vanished. He looked directly into her eyes, delving beneath the surface and reaching into her soul. Lynda had the uncomfortable feeling that he saw something she didn't even know herself. "I'm not entirely sure anymore," he admitted after a moment. "Except that I can't just drop whatever's started between us."

"Nothing's started between us," Lynda stated stubbornly. "Why can't you accept that?"

"Because it's not the truth," Kent returned. "Take my word on it, something's definitely started." After stopping at the traffic signal, he turned his full attention to her. "I also like to finish whatever I start."

Dear Reader:

So many of you asked for him, and now you've got him: Shiloh Butler, Mr. November. *Shiloh's Promise* by BJ James, is the long-awaited sequel to *Twice in a Lifetime*. Not only do many of your favorite characters reappear, but the enigmatic and compelling Shiloh now has his very own story—and his own woman!

And coming in December... *Wilderness Child* by Ann Major. This tie-in to her *Children of Destiny* series winds up 1989 in a very exciting way....

I've been telling you so much about the *Man of the Month* program that I want to mention some other exciting plans we have in store for you. Celeste Hamilton will be starting a trilogy in December with *The Diamond's Sparkle*. And the next few months will be bringing you Desires from such favorites as Katherine Granger, Linda Lael Miller and Dixie Browning....

So go wild with Desire—you'll be glad you did!

All the best,

Lucia Macro
Senior Editor

JANET
BIEBER

SEEING IS BELIEVING

SILHOUETTE *Desire*

Published by Silhouette Books New York

America's Publisher of Contemporary Romance

SILHOUETTE BOOKS
300 East 42nd St., New York, N.Y. 10017

ISBN: 0-373-05533-1

First Silhouette Books printing November 1989

Printed in the U.S.A.

Books by Janet Bieber

Silhouette Desire

Montana's Treasures #470
Seeing Is Believing #533

JANET BIEBER

admits to being a lifelong romantic and dreamer. However, she didn't even think of writing down all those dreams until she met a fellow romance addict. Fate took a hand, and a friendship and the writing collaboration "Janet Joyce" were born of that meeting. Since that day, she has authored or coauthored more than twenty contemporary and historical novels.

Her husband swept her off her feet more than twenty years ago, proving that white knights do exist in the twentieth century. Janet lives in Columbus, Ohio, with her husband, son and two daughters, an aging, gentle setter and a young, feisty cat. She says that when the chaos of three teenagers gets to be too much, she and the pets escape to her study, where the dog sleeps, Janet spins her dreams out via a word processor and the cat attacks the paper coming out of the printer.

For Jim,
my very special consultant,
who's taught me all I know
about vision and a lot of other things
and who even trims the hedges

Prologue

This would be the first Capital City Bank meeting to be held in the new building bearing the bank's name. A monument to the best of modern architecture, the building rose high above the center of Columbus. Three generations of Berringers assembled to take their places around the long mahogany table that had served the family for more than a century.

The decor was ultramodern everywhere but in the boardroom. There, the original boardroom—dark paneling, heavy damask drapes, a jewel-toned Oriental rug centered on the parquet floor where the leather-upholstered chairs surrounded the table—had been carefully duplicated as if to emphasize that Capital City Bank was an old, dependable and very conservative institution. Or maybe it had been recreated as a reminder to the youngest generation of Berringers of their heritage.

Kent Berringer noted that his sister, Theresa, took a look around the room before she slid into the chair carrying a small brass plaque with her name engraved on it. Sniffing the air, she winked at him. "Smells as stuffy as the old place," she whispered. "Suppose they scraped up some of the dust and scattered it around?"

"Probably. Uncle George wanted authenticity, and you know how thorough he is," Kent whispered into her ear as he pushed her chair in.

Unaware that he was the cause of his niece's snuffled giggle, George Berringer lifted a censorious brow at the two late arrivals. "Now that we're all assembled, the June meeting will begin. You all received copies of the report, and another has been provided in the portfolios before you. If you'll open them now, we'll start with the first item on the agenda."

With a rustling of paper, the assembly of twelve dutifully followed the directive, for to do otherwise would be unthinkable. Berringers were an orderly lot. Always had been. Always would be.

Kent dutifully extracted the designated page. His brows rose when he saw that the first item on the agenda was a decision on the artwork to be displayed in the lobby of the new building. After a quick judgment that either of the final choices, a mural of acrylic or one woven in textured yarns, was acceptable to him, he tuned out his uncle's opening remarks. He saw Theresa scribbling something in the margin of a page, then slide it to him.

Busy later this afternoon? I need a favor.

Experience prompted Kent to deny acquiescence until the exact nature of the favor was known. *What's the favor?*

Theresa's immediate answer was vague, as were the ones that followed.

Kent's wariness intensified with each scribbled reply. Stubbornly, he demanded specifics.

Assuming he had the assemblage's total attention, George continued on in his usual somnolent tones. Leaving out none of the details, he reiterated the process a committee had used to arrive at the final two works from the dozens originally submitted.

In reality, far more vigilance was being paid to the handsome raven-haired siblings and the sheet of paper veritably flying back and forth between them than to the sketches displayed on the two easels flanking George. Between each shift of the paper's location, Kent's vehement shake of his head was met with a pleading wide-eyed look from his sister.

Patricia Berringer, their mother, began to tap her meticulously manicured nails on the waxed surface of the table, accompanied by a pointed glare at her offspring. The glare was ignored, if it was even noticed.

Great-Aunt Edith was openly amused with the byplay, but then everyone knew she had a soft spot for Theresa and Kent in addition to the one suspected in her head. Great-Uncle Matthew kept shifting his gaze back and forth as if he were watching a tennis match. Cousin Russell hid his grin of amusement behind his hand. Cousin Carol cleared her throat, as if the sound would remind the two Berringer rebels where they were. The rest of the Berringers struck varying poses, all designed to give the impression that they were paying absolutely no attention to the goings on between Theresa and Kent.

George finished his recitation and called for a vote. For the acrylic or the weaving? Few of the conclave knew. "All those in agreement, signify by saying aye."

"I won't do it!" Kent's chair scraped back and toppled over as he jumped to his feet. "And that's final!"

George's reading glasses slipped farther down his nose. The usually unflappable man gaped at his nephew for a moment before he recovered. Calmly, he inquired, "Do you need more information, Kent?"

"I've got all the information I need," Kent growled, his cobalt glare directed at his sister before pandemonium broke, or as near that state as a gathering of the Berringer clan could approximate.

"Really, Kenton!" Patricia exclaimed.

Ignoring her mother and everyone else in the room, Theresa grinned mischievously at her brother. "And I've got all the information I need to make you do it."

"Theresa! Kenton!" Patricia's shrill pronouncement of her children's names cut above Edith's deep guffaw and the more sedate murmurs of the others. "What is the meaning of this?"

Theresa rose majestically from her chair, swished her waist-length black hair back over her shoulder and whispered something in her brother's ear.

Kent's eyes grew wider, then his face became a glowering mask of outrage. "Why you little black—"

"Ah...ah...ah," Theresa chided lightly. "Just calling in my markers. What do you say?"

Kent's neck turned a deep crimson as he reached for his fallen chair. "I'll do it," he pronounced between gritted teeth. He righted the chair and sat down once again.

"Uh-hum. All those in favor say aye," repeated the chairman of the august gathering.

The assemblage so signified, and when Theresa broke into a fit of laughter, her brother gave serious thought to fratricide.

One

Dr. Lynda Fisher shrank within the confines of her white lab jacket as another masculine garment flew her way. Her cheeks throbbed with the heat of the blush flaming over her ivory skin.

Despite her embarrassment, she couldn't keep her eyes away from the near-naked male body swaying rhythmically in the middle of the waiting room of Drs. Kelsey and Fisher. As if drawn by a powerful magnet, she watched the single droplet of perspiration that slithered slowly down the middle of the man's chest then coyly disappeared into the elastic band peeping through his open fly. The tip of her tongue had forced its way past her tightened lips before she shook her head and tore away the hypnotic veil that had settled over her.

The scream of Velcro parting company startled her. Defensively, she squeezed her eyes shut...but for only a split second. Red-blooded female curiosity impelled her lids to spring open. She gulped and her mouth went dry.

His pants were gone. Abruptly ripped apart at the Velcroed seams, the front had landed somewhere near the aquarium in the far corner of the room and the back was crumpled in a pool of black leather behind his bare feet.

Lynda's breath caught in her throat. The man's thighs were all muscle and sinew beneath a light haze of curling black hair. Even his feet, dancing across the sand-toned carpet, were sexy.

This show, display, or whatever you called it, had to be stopped.

But Lynda's primal instincts rose. She'd cut out the tongue of the first person who tried to call a halt to the show.

This was totally unprofessional and unethical, her civilized conscience argued. Could she lose her optometry license? How soon would the front door again bear only Dr. Kelsey's name? Thank God, Dr. Kelsey was still home recovering from his heart attack. This kind of a performance in the middle of his waiting room would have surely set his recovery back several weeks—or caused another attack.

She sent up further thanks that John, the office technician, and the young high school girl who worked as a file clerk after school weren't in the office, either. John would have been so embarrassed he might never have reported to work again. And Sherrie was only sixteen, far too young to witness anything like this.

Lynda should've stopped this . . . this show before it began. She should stop it now. But he was so good at the bumps and grinds.

Please God, let it be a dream.

God wasn't being merciful. Or, maybe He was being merciful. This man was every woman's fantasy. And he was her "gift."

Sexy music was blaring through the office intercom. A gorgeous man was removing his clothing a scant three feet away. There were patients and the majority of the building's receptionists seated with her in the office's waiting room.

How had they all known about it…him? She'd find out about that later. For whatever interminable length of time it would take for the man to complete his act, Lynda was going to try to endure.

And then she'd take out a contract on her sister. This…dancer had to be from Suzanne. Lynda's thirtieth birthday had provided the perfect excuse for Suzanne to launch the latest tactic in her campaign to loosen up her staid, older sister.

At that moment, Lynda was far from feeling loose. Every muscle in her body was so tight, she felt like an overloaded spring.

Everything had happened so fast. Lynda couldn't remember if she'd even seen the dancer's face before he started. Once his jacket, vest and shirt had gone, who'd cared about his face?

Lynda's range of vision was completely filled with flesh. Male flesh. Hard. Muscular. Bare and tanned. Six feet of it.

The flesh glistened. The muscles rippled across the broad chest and flat belly. What a chest and belly they were, decorated so enticingly by a perfect configuration of hair—growing wide across the chest and narrowing to a thin strip that drew the eye ever downward. The whole package belonged to a man, a mature, in-his-prime, perfect specimen of a man.

What gorgeous legs—especially those thighs! She wasn't sure if she'd expressed the thought aloud or not. She feared she had, for the exclamation had sounded too clearly to have been only in her head.

Lynda swallowed hard and squeezed her eyes shut again. God had shown a little mercy. This gyrating male body, posing initially as an optical-lab representative, hadn't descended on the office and swung into his act until five minutes before closing time.

There had been no children waiting. No men. Only a fifty-year-old businesswoman in for a pair of reading glasses, a mother to pick up a replacement contact lens for her teenager and the magically appearing five receptionists, only one of whom belonged in the offices of Kelsey and Fisher. And all of them, women from twenty to sixty, were cheering the man on!

A soft bundle landed on Lynda's clenched hands. Startled, she gasped as she stared in horror at the boxer shorts, still warm from body heat. They burned right through her linen skirt and scorched her thighs. Unconsciously, she crossed her legs and wound her ankles.

Fearful but unable to stop herself, she glanced at the man to see what remained. Not much. The leopard-print bikini-style briefs weren't nearly enough to come close to camouflaging the man's endowments.

Good grief! His thumbs were at the waistband. Lynda feared a vice-squad raid at any minute, but could she stop him? Not if her life depended on it.

A heated flush was spreading throughout her entire body, and a fine sheen of perspiration covered her skin.

And then it was over. The briefs were tossed in her lap. He wore only a red string bikini. He tossed Lynda a small card wishing her a happy birthday, courtesy of Terri's Tributes. Executing a sweeping bow, he disappeared into the inner office.

Lynda sagged into her chair.

"Wow!" Mrs. Goldman exclaimed, fanning her face with a magazine. "That was worth the price of replacing Chip's contact lens. You do this often here?"

"Every Friday," Jennifer Finch, Lynda's office manager/receptionist, vowed as she gathered up the garments scattered about the waiting room. With a leer, she picked up the briefs and dangled them before her audience. "We have a five-fifteen appointment open next week."

"Pencil me in!" chimed six feminine voices simultaneously.

Lynda looked around. Relief washed over her and erased some of her embarrassment when she realized that none of the other women were disgusted by what had just happened. By the expressions on their faces, they'd all enjoyed every minute of it.

And why not? They were innocent bystanders. Not one of them would be held accountable for what had just happened. She'd be the one who might lose everything if news of this filtered to the wrong places. The state board of optometry, for example, or the American Academy of Optometry. She'd never be accepted into the latter's elite membership. However, if she were at all lucky and Jennifer could be bribed to keep her mouth shut about the incident, nothing would happen.

Putting aside her concerns, Lynda tried gamely to enter into the fun. She chuckled nervously. "Sorry, I'm afraid that was a one-time show," she stated. "That sort of thing might cause eye strain."

She fielded several more comments and received birthday greetings from all before the office was cleared. Jennifer, the bundle of clothing tucked beneath her arm, disappeared through the swinging door that led to the interior of the office. Moments later, Lynda heard the click of the office's back door, and when Jennifer didn't reappear, she assumed the woman had made a hasty exit along with the performer.

"Afraid to face me, eh?" Lynda muttered under her breath, putting Jennifer at the top of the list of suspects who might have sent *that man* as a gift.

No, Lynda thought. Jennifer couldn't have been solely responsible. Lynda guessed that sort of gift came with a fairly sizeable price tag. Jennifer's salary supported herself and a college-aged daughter. The woman wasn't at all the kind of parent to squander her money.

The cost should have prevented Suzanne, but there was a lot of Papa in Suzanne. Gerald Fisher had been negligent in the rearing of his daughters in many ways, but celebrating birthdays hadn't been one of them. It was done as extravagantly as possible, often more than was prudent, considering the oftentimes shaky finances of the Fisher family.

Lynda grimaced. In the years since their father's death, she had thought she'd managed to teach her younger sister something about living within one's means. Evidently, the lessons hadn't completely taken hold.

It wasn't until Lynda was walking down the hall toward the refraction room to turn off the equipment and lights that she realized she wasn't alone in the office. Her private office door opened behind her and out stepped *the man*. At least Lynda assumed it was him, though now that he was fully clothed she wasn't sure.

She could have described every muscle on his torso, the way his body moved, the color of his skin, the configuration of the hair on his chest, even his scent— a fresh crisp fragrance with an undeniably male edge. But his face? He might as well have had a hood over his head for all she knew about it. Not once during the dance had she been able to look above his neck.

She did now.

Blue eyes, the truest blue she'd ever seen, stared straight into hers. A swath of ebony hair fell across his wide square forehead. High cheekbones.

And what a mouth. Wide, sensual, the lower lip fuller than the upper. A little tight around the edges, and was that rosy color creeping up from his neck?

He was embarrassed. The man who'd just stripped unabashedly down to almost nothing in front of eight women was embarrassed to run into only one of them with all his clothes on!

"I didn't know—"

"I didn't know—"

Their two voices, a smooth baritone and a husky alto, chorused. Despite her own discomfort, Lynda laughed. Instead of joining her, the man flushed a deeper red. His gaze was directed to a spot beyond Lynda's head.

"Sorry. I thought I'd be able to sneak out without running into anyone," he confessed sheepishly, shifting his gym bag to his other hand.

In the light of his obvious discomfort, Lynda's evaporated. "Haven't you another card for me?" She was sure that the card she was requesting would bear her sister's flamboyant signature.

"The giver wishes to remain anonymous." He kept his gaze indirect.

The sound that erupted from Lynda was a combination derisive snort and hooting laugh. "That's hard to believe," she said under her breath. Never had her uninhibited little sister avoided taking credit for something so audacious. Lynda considered crossing Suzanne's name off the list of suspects.

"Look, this has gone on long enough," Lynda stated, holding her hand out palm up. "Give me the card."

"You already have one," was the gruff response. "At the end of my act, I tossed it in your lap."

"But there has to be—" The man's slow shake of his head stopped her. The belligerent set of his jaw eroded her conviction that he'd divulge the identity of the responsible party, but she was determined to find out. Though she wasn't a practical joker, she'd had plenty of experience growing up with a father who'd been one, and she wasn't one to walk away from the challenge of retribution.

"Give me a name," she ordered.

His gaze swung directly to her, its intensity threatening the brittle poise she'd assumed. "I'm prohibited from giving out the name of the giver," he told her blandly.

"You were certainly uninhibited enough to take off all your clothes a few minutes ago. Why have you suddenly developed scruples?"

The scowl that appeared on his face was dark enough to force Lynda to take a step backward. "What makes you think I don't have any scruples?" he inquired with a growl.

Attacking this man's character was a definite mistake. After all, he'd only been doing his job, such as it was. It wasn't any of her business how he chose to make a living.

Looking at the ceiling, Lynda took a deep breath. "Look, I'm sorry. I'm just not used to—"

"Seeing a naked man," he finished for her, punctuating the statement with a deep chuckle.

It was a knowing sound, purely male, and Lynda blushed. Without thinking she blurted, "I've seen naked men before!"

His chuckle grew heartier and more taunting. "Got a subscription to *Playgirl* have you?"

"I most certainly do not!"

He grinned, and from the depths of his eyes glimmered a flash of mischief. "Why, Dr. Fisher, are you admitting to some hands-on experience?"

Lynda choked down an exasperated "Oh!" Fists clenched at her sides, she gathered the shreds of professional dignity and straightened her spine.

Drawing up all of her sixty-five inches and hoping she projected at least six more, she replied coldly, "The door to the reception room is to your immediate left. The door to the outer hallway is still unlocked. Good day!"

Not budging an inch, he commented, "It has been, hasn't it?"

His smile revealed a mouthful of white teeth, straight, strong, positively dazzling in their gleaming perfection. Possibly under different circumstances Lynda would have described the smile as charming. Unfortunately, at that moment she felt a bit like Red Riding Hood facing the wolf.

"That is a matter of opinion. Will you kindly leave before I call the...the..."

Who did one call for assistance in this situation? The professional building didn't have a security guard, and the chances of hailing a policeman who might be cruising by the building were nil. "Leave now, and I won't report you to your superior or your company to the Better Business Bureau."

Even to her own ears, the threat was weak. The man outweighed her by at least seventy pounds of well-developed muscle. She was completely alone in the office and any escape was blocked. I should be scared to death, she thought, as she glared up at the man. She wasn't.

For some reason, she didn't think this man would harm her physically. Eyes were her profession, and his didn't seem to reflect any malice. One long look from those cobalt depths might shatter her nerves, raise her blood pressure and demolish her poise, but real harm? She'd bet her expensive new ophthalmoscope against it.

Leaning against the wall, Lynda let out a long sigh. If the man had scruples, then it followed that he had compassion. "Look, it's been a long day, and I still have some paperwork to finish up. You've done what you were hired to do. Just leave me in peace."

That mischief in his eyes disappeared as his eyebrows arched. "It's past six o'clock, lady. You ought to go home," he said with what sounded like genuine concern.

"I can't. I still have some work to do." Pushing away from the wall, she reached in her coat pocket for her keys and jingled them. "Come on. Get moving. I'll lock up after you."

"You're going to work late on your birthday?" he asked with such incredulity that Lynda felt as if he'd just accused her of blasphemy.

"The work has to be done, and I'm the only one who can do it," she explained, sounding far more defensive than she would have liked. She didn't have to rationalize her work habits to anyone, especially not this man.

"I find it much easier to finish up patient records and fill out the lab orders at the end of the day when the office is quiet," Lynda surprised herself by continuing. "It gives me a chance to collect my thoughts without any interruption."

"I suppose I can understand that, but it's your birthday," he insisted. "Surely you're going to celebrate this momentous occasion."

It had been momentous all right, she thought. Anything further would be anticlimactic, and she caught herself just in time from telling him so. "Look, if you must know, I do have plans this evening for a very quiet little dinner with friends."

"Friends? A special friend? A man, perhaps?"

Bristling at the implication that she couldn't be happy without a special man in her life, Lynda wanted to tell him exactly what she thought. Instead, she heard herself say, "Well, if you must know, there will be a special man at my birthday dinner. Dr. William Kelsey will be there and . . . and we're very close."

Lynda couldn't believe her own ears. She'd just implied that she and dear Dr. Kelsey, her mentor, a man almost old enough to be her grandfather, had something going. Furious with herself for letting herself be baited into telling such a whopper, she hurried on, unable to meet the man's eyes. "A few friends and my sister—perfect company to celebrate my birthday with. And if you don't get out of here, I won't be able to get my work done and I'll be late."

Deciding the end of this conversation was long overdue, Lynda started to move around him.

He smoothly took up more space so that she was unable to pass. She was forced to retreat, but she was far from surrendering. Conjuring up what she hoped was a chilling glare, she looked up at him.

He was staring at her as if she'd sprouted a second head. "You and Dr. Kelsey? The other optometrist in this office?" he asked, his tone conveying some skepticism.

Lynda gulped. Good old Murphy's law was in force. Lynda Fisher told a lie and was immediately caught. It never failed.

Yet it wasn't really a lie. She and Dr. Kelsey were very close. She'd known him most of her life. He'd been the one who'd encouraged her during her college years, then believed in her so strongly that he'd taken her on as an associate immediately after her graduation. And he'd been married for more than forty years to a lovely woman whose friendship Lynda held dear.

Squaring her shoulders, she asserted, "Yes, Dr. Kelsey and I are very close."

He tilted his head slightly and lifted one eyebrow. The corners of his mouth were twitching slightly, and

Lynda held her breath, waiting for his laughter. It would be just her luck that he knew Dr. Kelsey.

To her relief, he finally stepped aside, and she let out her breath as quietly as possible as she led the way to the exit. Trailing closely behind her, he asked, "Still going to put in some work time?"

Lynda nodded.

"No wonder somebody sent you a strip-o-gram. All work and no play make—"

"A successful practice," she finished crisply. Her hand on the knob, she turned and faced him. "Since, for obvious reasons, I'll be unable to do so, please express my thanks to my anonymous donor. You gave quite a performance, Mr...."

When he didn't immediately supply a name, Lynda's curiosity was aroused. She studied his features more closely. No mischief was sparkling in his eyes, which didn't quite meet hers. No color rising at his collar, but he was definitely uncomfortable.

"You do have a name, don't you?" she prompted.

"Sure I have a name. It's...it's..." He paused, obviously searching.

Lynda frowned. He was holding out on her. She supposed if she was in his line of work, she wouldn't want to divulge her name, either. But surely he had some sort of pseudonym he used in his profession, something suitably fitting like Flash or Lash or Zip. Leaning against the door, this time being the escape blocker, she again prompted, "Well?"

"It's...ah...Slide. Slide Hornblower."

After a second of stunned silence, Lynda exploded into laughter. "Slide Hornblower? Worse than I thought," she said.

Tears were streaming down her face by the time she brought her laughter under control. Swiping at her eyes with her hands, she peered up at Slide, for the first time noticing that he hadn't joined her in laughter. Lynda's last remaining giggles died in her throat.

"I have the feeling you don't laugh often enough," he said. "Maybe that's why someone ordered the strip-o-gram. They must have hoped to put a smile on your face and laughter in your big brown eyes."

Uncomfortable under a gaze that definitely delved deeper than she wanted, Lynda sobered completely. "Well, ah... it's been quite a day. I'm afraid I've reached the hysterical level. I haven't laughed like this in years."

"Too bad. Your mouth was designed for laughter and..." His voice, already low and husky, trailed off, and his eyes fixed solidly on her mouth.

Lynda caught her breath, then cleared her throat. "I believe you were about to leave, Mr. Hornblower," she said pointedly. Reaching behind her, she turned the knob and started to pull the door open.

Without warning, he reached past her shoulder and pushed the door closed. Curling his arm around her waist, he pulled her tightly against him. Before Lynda could utter more than a startled squeak, she was imprisoned within his arms. "Just curious," he said just before his lips covered hers gently.

In shock, Lynda swayed forward, inadvertently pressing her lips against his. He must have taken it as a signal to deepen the possession, for his mouth hardened and demanded a response. On a level far removed from conscious thought, Lynda gave the answer Slide sought.

She opened her mouth and moaned softly when his tongue slid beyond the barrier of her teeth. Sweeping through like a conqueror, he explored every crevice and returned the pleasure full measure. His fingers caressed the length of her spine. Lynda's entire body throbbed when he wrapped her closer, and the beat of his heart merged with her own.

As suddenly as the kiss had begun, it stopped. Dropping his arms, Slide lifted his head and stepped away. "Lady, you're a fraud," he pronounced, his voice low and intimate in its gruffness. "One of these days you and I are going to be even."

"Even?" Lynda managed to whisper.

"Even." He grinned, then planted a quick kiss on her lips. "Happy birthday, Dr. Fisher. My birthday's coming up soon. I'll be seeing you...."

Two

———

Kent tossed the gym bag holding the Velcro-seamed pants and the skimpy underwear in the general direction of the reception desk. "All debts past and future are paid, little sister!"

Theresa grinned. "Oh, I don't know. Not telling the clan about the time you substituted at Chippendale's ought to be worth more than one favor."

"Stop right there, you little blackmailer! I subbed in the *band* at Chippendale's." With his fists on the desk, Kent loomed over her. With gritted teeth, he declared, "I was not one of the featured performers."

"It's no secret you had some pretty lean times back when you were on the road with that first band you put together after high school. You were still a growing boy," she teased. "It stands to reason you might have taken off your clothes for a meal."

"I was never that desperate."

Theresa's dimples didn't fade. "What if news of your, uh, little performance this afternoon got out...say to a few parties at Switzer, Smith and Hazlebaker?" she asked, naming the law firm where Kent was in line for a partnership.

"If news of my performance should reach the wrong ears, it'll be quickly followed by the details of the time you spent the night in the boardroom with Andy Fredericks." Kent looked appraisingly around the attractive office of Terri's Tributes. "I doubt it would have any effect on this business, but Uncle George would never forgive you for turning the holy of holies into a love nest. Why, even Aunt Edith would be upset."

His grin was one of triumph rather than mirth. He knew his little sister well. She might commit a few off-the-wall actions by Berringer standards, but she drew the line at out and out shocking the family.

Theresa's dimples had disappeared. "But...that was years ago...and nothing happened. I was just showing him around the place, and then that stupid old door got stuck. We killed time playing chess until you came and rescued us."

"A detail I'll leave out if you ever leave out the realities of my short stint at Chippendale's." Having delivered the *coup de grace*, he pushed away from the desk and stood upright.

If he'd remembered that incident earlier in the day, he would have saved himself a lot of trouble and embarrassment. But then he might never have met Lynda Fisher. Kissing the birthday girl had been a very gratifying fringe benefit, even more gratifying than wiping the grin off his sister's face. But that kiss had not only been gratifying, it had been stupendous. He'd done it purely on impulse and to satisfy an overwhelming need to crack through the stiff facade Lynda had put up when she'd shown him the door.

If her response was any indication, he'd made a big crack in her facade. That kiss had been a shared experience. She'd responded, then initiated as much as he had. Lynda Fisher had seen the last of Slide Hornblower, but she was going to meet Kent Berringer soon—and she was going to see a lot of him. The more he thought about it, the more he thought maybe Theresa had done him a favor.

Clearing her throat, Theresa leaned back in her chair. "So, how did this afternoon go?" she asked nonchalantly.

Remembering the shock on Lynda's face during his performance and then the third degree she'd tried to implement afterward, Kent stiffened. He was going to have to come up with some fancy footwork to undo the damage done by the circumstances of that first meeting. "It went fine, just fine. But you'll have to cancel the next call for a male stripper unless your regular boy can do it."

"No problem. Look, I really do appreciate what you did for me."

The bell over the door tinkled merrily, and they both turned to see who was coming in so late. The handsome young man who was Theresa's regular stripper sauntered into the reception room.

Kent took a long assessing look at the healthy college student who was supposed to be at death's door. "Theresa . . . ?"

Lynda closed the file folder she'd been staring at. It was no use trying to get any work done. Her concentration was nil. She couldn't even read. Every time she looked at an exam form, she saw deep cobalt-blue eyes instead. And then her lips would go dry, and she'd lick them, and they'd start pulsing again, and she'd remember every second of that kiss.

Blowing out some of her frustration, she shook her head. She had almost an hour before her birthday celebration. The relaxing evening Lynda had been looking forward to was showing promise of being anything but.

She massaged her throbbing temples. She'd worked so hard, and she was afraid to have success snatched away at the last minute. Memories of past disappointments flooded her, followed quickly by a too-familiar knot in her stomach.

Before the sting of tears behind her eyes turned into a waterfall down her face, Lynda got herself in hand. The stripper had been somebody's idea of a joke. Even though the culprit was no doubt her own sister, Lynda, herself, hadn't been responsible for it . . . him. Dr. Kelsey had a sense of humor. He'd understand.

Holding that thought, she hung up her lab jacket and freshened up for the evening. Her best defense against Suzanne's prank was to give at least an outward appearance of being totally unruffled. After splashing water on her face, she renewed what little makeup she wore and added a little extra eye shadow and blusher. A light spray of cologne, a few strokes through her hair with a brush, and she felt, if not refreshed, at least better.

"You're not responsible for anybody's actions but your own," she repeated to herself as she went back to her desk. "Not even those of a family member."

But you could've stopped it, her conscience re-minded.

No red-blooded woman in her right mind would have stopped it, her more primitive side defended.

But... It is your birthday, and you deserve to cele-brate. You've done a lot in your thirty years, her con-science relented.

"I do deserve to celebrate," Lynda remarked aloud. It wasn't rationalizing but a statement of fact when she reminded herself that it had been darned hard getting through undergraduate, then professional school with the little her father had left her and no one but Su-zanne and Dr. Kelsey to encourage her. If all contin-ued to go well, Dr. Kelsey would be selling his practice to her when he retired.

"If I continue to work hard," she reminded herself as she pulled open a bottom drawer of her desk and exchanged her comfortable low-heeled shoes for a pair of slender-heeled patent leather pumps.

"I will. Not even the eccentricities of a family member will stop me," she declared, replacing the leather belt she'd worn at her waist all day with the scarf that had draped around the V-neck of her sheath dress.

With a last look in a mirror, she was impressed by the transformation. "From office smart to evening chic with a few minor adjustments," a sales clerk had promised, and Lynda had to agree. She was ready for the evening in appearance and determined to use the driving time to the restaurant to formulate a plan to force Suzanne's confession about sending the gift.

William Kelsey lifted his champagne flute and toasted, "To the best associate I've ever had. I don't know how I ever got along without you. Many happy returns of the day, my dear colleague."

A lump formed in Lynda's throat, preventing her from saying more than "Thank you." She respected Dr. Kelsey more than anyone in the profession. For him to call her his colleague was high praise indeed.

Suzanne and her date, Jay Holland, added their own best wishes.

Lynda nodded and smiled, watching her sister closely. The evening was close to a half hour old, and so far Suzanne's behavior and comments had remained completely guileless. Lynda began to consider taking her off the suspect list.

Grace Kelsey lifted her glass. The gentle gray-haired woman smiled warmly. "Happy birthday, Lynda. Thank you for all you've done in the last months and for being the wonderful young woman you are," she stated sincerely. Her eyes sparkled with unshed tears when she squeezed her husband's arm. "I might not still have this guy if he'd had to worry about his practice. We both owe you so much. Not just for keeping the practice going, but for all the time you spent with Bill and all those hours you held my hand."

"It is I who owe you," Lynda responded. "Taking over during Dr. Kelsey's recuperation was small payment for all you've done for me," she said. Then, because she felt uncomfortable under such an onslaught of praise, she diverted the conversation to another subject—Trafalgar Square, the new supper club that was the site of their little celebration. The establishment had a pleasant atmosphere—sophisticated but inviting—a gourmet menu and it promised Lynda's favorite music—jazz. The evening was nothing short of perfect. Good company, relaxing ambiance, good food. The music would be the icing on the cake.

Lynda was savoring the last of her meal when the sound of the musicians tuning up reached her ears. Like nearly everyone else, she turned her attention eagerly toward the low, curved stage at the opposite side of the dining room.

A trombone held in his hand, the leader had his back to the patrons while he made some inaudible comments to the other musicians. Lynda was already admiring the breadth of the man's shoulders and the narrowness of his hips when Jay leaned toward her. "Wait till he starts to play. Suzanne told me you love jazz. You're in for a treat tonight."

"You've heard this group before?" Lynda inquired.

"From its beginnings. The trombone player is an old friend of mine. He and I go way back. We used to—"

The rest of Jay's statement was lost on Lynda when the man in question turned to his audience and brought the instrument to his lips. *Slide!*

Lynda froze for a few seconds. When her body began to work again, she gasped for breath. She emptied her champagne glass with one gulp, squeezing her eyes shut to the bubbles.

Hoping that it was all just a bad dream, she opened her eyes and glanced toward the musicians. He was still there. Legs bent, spine curving back, his eyes closed as he wrought mellow tones from his instrument, he was completely unaware of the turmoil he was causing in her.

Slide Hornblower! She would have laughed out loud at the man's pseudonym, but the last thing she wanted was to call attention to herself. Instead, she shrunk into her soft chair and prayed for invisibility while she waited for Suzanne to start hooting in triumph. A glance showed that her sister was showing no sign of doing so. Either she'd become a very good actress or she was innocent.

Lynda prepared to bolt as soon as possible. There was bound to be some commotion when the group finished its first set. She'd make her exit then. For now, she'd endure.

Someone refilled her champagne glass, and she reached for it with gratitude. Far more circumspectly this time, she sipped the contents, giving an appearance of savoring the fine vintage. Settling back in her chair, the glass rarely out of her hand, she let herself concentrate on the music.

The quintet was good. Slide was fantastic. Obviously, a man of many talents, Lynda thought cynically.

Suzanne leaned over and whispered, "Isn't he wonderful?"

Lynda felt chilled. This was it. The moment of truth. She braced herself.

Suzanne said nothing more, her attention fully on the band.

The music went on and on. And the contents of Lynda's champagne glass went on and on. The glass was seemingly bottomless, for she was sure she was steadily consuming it.

At last, when the final strains of Henry Mancini's immortal "Dreamsville" died away, the lights came up. The audience burst into applause, and Lynda grabbed her purse.

She literally jumped to her feet, then sank back in her chair. The room swam, and Lynda noticed that her sister and Jay had disappeared.

Mustering every ounce of control, she rose slowly and steadily to her feet. "Dr. Kelsey, Grace, it's been a lovely evening, but I'm afraid I'll have to call it a night. Early day tomorrow. I'll thank Suzanne and Jay later."

"Thank us for what?" Suzanne inquired, reappearing as suddenly as she'd disappeared.

Lynda dropped limply back into her chair. Suzanne and Jay weren't alone. *He* was with them and being introduced to everyone. "My friend, Kent Berringer," Jay was saying.

With a smile guaranteed to melt icebergs, Kent reached for Lynda's hand, brought it to his lips and brushed a kiss across it. "I understand it's your birthday. Might I have this dance?"

In a daze, Lynda heard the urging of the Kelseys and her sister and felt the gentle but firm pull on her hand. Within seconds, she was in Kent's arms and being guided around the dance floor in time with the recorded music played during the musicians' break. Kent was a good dancer, but then he had a lot of practice, didn't he?

Kent would have had to have been made of wood not to be aware of Lynda's stiff movements. Theresa had sworn that she and Suzanne hadn't told anybody about this afternoon's caper, so Jay had no way of knowing how ill-timed tonight's introduction to Lynda was.

He swore inwardly. He'd hoped to let the memory of this afternoon fade a bit more before seeing her again. Luck was not working in his corner this day.

"Of all the bizarre ways to meet someone, this one takes the prize," he stated, hoping to break through the ice that Lynda had thrown up around herself.

"Which meeting?" Lynda's low husky voice had entranced him that afternoon, but now it had a sharper edge. "This evening's or this afternoon's?" she asked.

"Let's forget this afternoon's, shall we?"

"Afraid your friends might be shocked?" Lynda asked, her gaze steadfastly fixed beyond Kent's shoulder.

Kent chuckled. Leaning back so that Lynda had no choice but to look at him, he shook his head. "It would take more than that to shock Jay. But it did shock you, and I'm sorry about that."

"But wasn't your performance meant to shock, to titillate?" Lynda gibed sarcastically, and went back to looking over Kent's shoulder. Anything to avoid looking at his face.

Unable to help himself, Kent asked, "Did you find my . . . ah . . . performance titillating?"

Lynda gasped and tried to pull out of his arms.

He tightened his grasp, smiling charmingly all the while. No one watching would guess that a small battle was going on between them.

"You did, didn't you?" he taunted for the fun of seeing her reaction rather than a need for an answer.

"I did not!" she declared indignantly.

"Like I said this afternoon, lady, you're a fraud," he maintained with a grin that challenged her to wipe it off his face.

"I am not, nor have I ever been a fraud," she stated firmly. "I am exactly what I present to the world."

Leaning backward, Kent forced her to look at him again. "What about you and your Dr. Kelsey?" he queried. "According to the introductions, that's his wife sitting beside him. You're one cool lady, Dr. Fisher. And you accuse me of having no scruples."

"I didn't claim that there was anything going on between Dr. Kelsey and me, only that we were close. And we, and I include Grace in that, *are* close," she insisted. "You jumped to the wrong conclusion."

"I'm not unique in that," he muttered. Then he challenged, "So exactly who are you, Lynda Fisher?"

"Nothing mysterious. The woman you entertained this afternoon is who I am."

"A hardworking, very serious professional?" He arched his eyebrows.

"Exactly."

He subjected her to another long delving gaze before folding their clasped hands against his chest and pulling her closer. He murmured into her hair, "But you're so much more than that. There's a warm, passionate woman underneath that no-nonsense manner of yours. Why do you hide yourself like that?"

Pulling her head away from his, Lynda restated her case. "Why should you care?"

"Let's just say I'm intrigued. Aren't you?"

"About you? No."

"Of course, you are. You couldn't help but be. Especially after that kiss we shared," Kent stated, hoping to lead into an explanation of his performance.

"You are the most egotistical man I've ever met!" Lynda meant every word and then some.

"I have to be in my business. It takes a certain amount of ego to perform in front of a crowd."

She couldn't believe her ears. She couldn't believe she was having this conversation. "You call it 'ego'? I'd call it a bad case of exhibitionism."

"I was talking about my band," he said coolly. "It takes some ego to stand out there playing the lead, believing that I'm pleasing the crowd."

Lynda felt a trifle foolish. A need for an ego when playing music for a crowd made sense. The musician in him, she could understand. "You're good. Very good," she complimented very sincerely. "One of the best I've ever heard."

"Thank you," he said humbly. "Now, about this afternoon . . ."

"Yes, this afternoon," she repeated sharply. "How could a man with all your talents do a thing like that? You have such gifts, stature as—"

"Stature?" he echoed belligerently. Alarm bells sounded through his head, and he stopped dancing. "Exactly what do you mean by that?"

"I think you know exactly what I mean, Kent Berringer," she accused, unwittingly fueling his rage. "But, if I need to spell it out for you here goes. How could such a gifted musician moonlight as a stripper? Have you no pride, self-respect, respect for. . .for your family?"

For a moment, he'd thought she'd been referring to his stature as a Berringer. That damned name. With it came a responsibility to "conduct himself above the rabble," according to the Berringer gospel, as interpreted by his mother. A Berringer never forgot that he was one of "those Berringers." If his mother had her way, no one would suspect her children were even human.

He'd wanted to shock Lynda Fisher and break through her armor. This was a perfect chance. It was perverse, but he decided against giving her any excuse for his performance. So this afternoon he'd been a male stripper. There are worse things. "Performing a strip-o-gram is lawful, and it gave me something to do this afternoon."

Lynda's mouth formed a perfect O. And then she laughed. It wasn't a sound filled with joy, but with disdain. "That's why you do it? For something to fill the time? I should think a man like you could find far more respectable uses for an idle afternoon."

"A man like me?" His tone was freezing, his eyes cutting coldly through her.

Lynda shrank beneath the intensity. Her accusation had struck a nerve, and his reaction was what it had been when she'd accused him of having no scruples. She wasn't about to apologize for she believed he was deserving of the accusation, but she certainly didn't want to remain in his arms or anywhere near his company. He'd used that hungry-lion growl again, and she had no desire to be his meal.

Pushing against his chest, she tried to extricate herself, but his grip around her waist tightened. "You're not getting away this soon, lady."

The music had stopped not long after Kent had stopped dancing. The pause was over, and another piece was beginning. Immediately, Kent swept Lynda into some fast, swirling moves that forced her to cling to him or risk tumbling them both to the floor.

Then Kent slowed their movements. Nuzzling her ear, he whispered, "Were you?"

"Was I what?" she managed, still breathless.

"Titillated this afternoon?" he queried, the lion growl replaced by playfulness.

Confusion over his change in mood and his question reigned until she remembered the way she'd described his performance. "No!" Her answer came out too loud and too defensive to be believed.

"Oh, come on, be honest," he urged, his breath blowing over her ear.

Lynda shivered. Convinced he was toying with her, she shrank as far away from him as she could. "Would you kindly give me some breathing space?" she demanded, striving not to sound defensive.

"You're breathing just fine. I'm aware of every breath you're taking."

She was sure he was aware of a lot more, for she'd registered more about him than the rhythmic expansion of his chest. He had molded her to him, and there seemed to be nothing she could do but endure. She prayed the music would end soon. Was it her imagination, or was this the longest piece of music on record?

"You're awfully quiet," he stated softly, again in her ear. "Trying to think up a description of your reaction to my performance this afternoon?"

Jerking her head away from him, she put a little distance between her ear and his mouth. "I was furious."

"And," he prodded, his grin full of the male knowing he'd displayed at their first confrontation.

Exasperated, she blurted angrily, "Oh, all right. I was titillated. If you need your ego stroked further, I'll even compliment you. You've got a great body and know how to move it. You were good, very good.

Every move appealed to the primal female urges, and I am a woman."

"You certainly are," he agreed, satisfaction clear in his voice. "But I wonder how often you remember."

He then fit her so closely to him that they were essentially two parts of a puzzle. As if this afternoon hadn't been enough, he was giving her a refresher course in all the differences between males and females. Lynda was having no trouble remembering.

Three

―――

Good morning, Dr. Fisher," Jennifer greeted cheerfully, placing a steaming mug of coffee on the counter beside the receptionist's station.

"Morning, and thanks," Lynda mumbled, reaching blindly for the mug as she perused the schedule.

"Light and easy this morning," Jennifer chirped. "Your first patient's not due for another twenty minutes, and if all goes smoothly, we could be finished by eleven."

"Smooth and uneventful would be nice." Lynda sipped at her coffee. Normally, she waited for her first swallow until she was out of Jennifer's range of vision and had weakened the strong brew with a liberal amount of water. This morning, a full-strength dose was needed to clear her fuzzy mind of the effects of too much champagne and not enough sleep.

Jennifer lowered her voice. "Quit worrying, dear," she offered gently and quietly. "No one, least of all Dr. Kelsey, will think any less of you because of what happened here yesterday. It was really harmless and somebody's idea of fun."

"I suppose it was," Lynda returned with surface resignation. Internally, she groaned. Harmless?

If Jennifer only knew the rest of the story. Lynda was thankful Jennifer hadn't been present the previous evening. She'd never let her forget what had happened.

Yesterday afternoon's performance was only the tip of the iceberg, an event that was harmless. However, Kent Berringer's actions of last night were anything but harmless.

As if he hadn't humiliated her enough by practically making love to her on the dance floor, he'd bent her over his arm and kissed her in front of everyone when he'd taken her back to her table. Lynda took another healthy swallow of coffee, shuddering less from the bitterness that assaulted her taste buds than from the memories of the raised eyebrows and smirks that she'd suffered through.

By leaving the restaurant almost immediately after that kiss, she'd avoided any discussion of the incident right then. She'd driven straight home, dismissed Suzanne's baby-sitter, then gone directly to bed. This morning, she'd evaded any discussion with Suzanne again by purposely arriving late for breakfast and directing her attention solely on her nieces.

Full of their usual morning exuberance, the pixie miniatures of their mother had happily dominated the few minutes Lynda had taken to wash down a piece of toast with a glass of orange juice. "We're going to give bubble baths to dogs,'' announced four-year-old Maureen before she burst into giggles.

Though obviously just as excited about the prospect of accompanying their mother to the veterinarian's office where she worked, five-year-old Ariel cautioned, ''Settle down, Moe, before you knock over the juice.''

''We're going to clean their houses, too. With a water hose,'' Moe elaborated. ''And we get to wear our bathing suits, right, Arrie?''

''But not the new ones, 'cause we're going to be doing hard, messy work.''

Despite her dark mood, Lynda couldn't help but laugh as she imagined just where the water hose was going to be directed most of the time. ''Maybe your mommy better wear her suit, too,'' she'd suggested as she rinsed out her glass. ''You all have a good time and I'll see you this evening.'' After a wave to her sister and hurried kisses on the top of the girls' shiny blond heads, Lynda had stepped out the door.

This rush through breakfast wasn't at all the way Lynda liked to start her day, and she chalked up one more black mark against Mr. Kent Berringer. Normally, she gave herself plenty of time for a leisurely breakfast with the family. She loved the morning meal with Suzanne and the girls, especially the girls. Working so many extra hours for the past few months, she rarely saw them any other time of the day, and she treasured those minutes at breakfast. Resolving to make it up to them and herself by spending time with them later that evening, she focused on the day ahead.

''As light as the schedule is,'' Lynda said to Jennifer, ''why don't you free Sherrie out of the file room and let her take over the front desk this morning.

That'll give you a chance to make friends with that new computerized patient recall system. After John does the prelims on Mr. Murillo, tell him to give me a buzz on the intercom.''

Scooping up a stack of invoices, she stepped across the hallway to the laboratory. Work. She'd immerse herself in it and be able to block out all the images that had kept her tossing and turning most of the night.

The ''light and easy'' schedule turned into a string of minor disasters, making it the worst Saturday morning Lynda had experienced since she'd begun practicing. During the first exam, the light bulb blew in the acuity-chart projector. It should have been a minor problem, easily remedied with one of the spares kept for just such an occurrence, except that Lynda dropped the burned-out bulb on the floor, where it shattered. The clean up set her several minutes behind schedule.

During the second exam, the power went off in the building and remained off for twenty minutes. Her patient took the inconvenience with good humor, but Lynda was beginning to suspect that the fates were massing a campaign against her and that she should have stayed home in bed.

Then, what should have been a very routine dispensing of eyewear turned sour. As calmly and politely as she could, Lynda dealt with the belligerent patient. Ushering him out, she took some solace in the knowledge that she had handled the situation as Dr. Kelsey would have.

Rubbing the pain that was throbbing at her temples, Lynda whispered to Sherrie, ''I'm going to take a short break. Tell John to take his time doing the prelims on the next patient, will you?''

"No problem," Sherrie assured, her face flushed and her eyes unusually bright. "I'll be happy to take him back to the preliminary exam room myself. Oooo, Dr. Fisher, wait until you see this guy. He's a real hunk."

"As long as he's the last patient of the day, I don't care if he's a hunchback," Lynda said, and went into the lavatory.

Vowing she'd never touch champagne the rest of her life, Lynda downed two aspirin then turned on the tap. Running warm water over her wrists and exercising some simple meditation techniques relaxed her.

Fifteen minutes later, feeling considerably better, Lynda headed toward the exam room. She picked up the folder in the rack and read the name as she went through the door. Berringer, Kenton J. She froze in midstride and looked again, sure she'd misread the name. She hadn't.

She stepped back into the hall. Could it be a coincidence? Maybe Kenton J. Berringer wasn't that Kent Berringer.

Jennifer's voice drifted through the doorway, but Lynda didn't have long to wonder why the reception-ist was chatting with one of the patients in the exam room. His voice rumbled in response to whatever Jennifer had said. For one moment, Lynda consid-ered marching out of the office. But then, pride took over.

That man was not in the office for any legitimate reason, but she'd play this little game, at least until they were alone. Not for anything was she going to let Jennifer know she was suspicious of Kent Berringer's motives for being in the office this morning. The middle-aged matchmaker would have a heyday.

Her shoulders straight, her greet-the-new-patient smile on her face, Lynda entered the room. Extending her hand, she said, "Hello, Mr. Berringer. I'm Dr. Fisher."

Amusement sparkling in his eyes, Kent grasped her hand, and wasn't surprised when she pulled it away quickly. "Dr. Fisher." Turning his attention back to Jennifer, he smiled engagingly and said, "Thanks again for slipping me in at the last minute. I really needed this appointment."

I'll just bet you did, Lynda thought, glaring at him. She pretended to study the patient information form, as Jennifer stepped out. When the older woman was well out of earshot, Lynda crossed her arms over her chest, leaned against the wall and fixed Kent with a steady glare. "Exactly why are you here, Mr. Berringer?"

"I need my vision checked," Kent answered smoothly, his expression perfectly innocent. "Can you think of any other reason I'd be here?"

Nonplussed, Lynda continued to stare at him until she recovered her poise. She sat on the stool she used during examinations and resumed her professional role. "There is absolutely no other reason why you'd be here," she stated firmly, returning her attention to the examination form.

Within the space of thirty seconds, she knew his age, thirty-six; his health status, good; and that there was absolutely nothing in his history or the preliminary findings to warrant any concern, except that he was slightly far-sighted.

"Everything looks pretty normal so far, Mr. Berringer," Lynda remarked as she flicked off the overhead light and reached for her ophthalmoscope.

"Your visual fields, color vision and the glaucoma test revealed nothing out of the ordinary," she said matter-of-factly. Armoring herself against being further affected by his presence, she prepared for the proximity of heads necessary for the proper study of the interior of the eye.

"Look to the far end of the room," she directed as she leaned forward, wishing her instrument was a far larger shield between herself and this disturbing man. What she saw with the tiny light was textbook perfect. What else had she expected? She already had ample proof that this man was as perfect a specimen as could be found on earth.

He also smelled wonderful—soap and a faint touch of some guaranteed knock-'em-dead cologne mixed with his own natural scent. Lynda felt her body tighten and warm in all the places that identified her as a woman. That his forehead was separated by less than a centimeter from hers and their mouths by mere inches didn't help matters any.

Though unnerved, Lynda was determined to brazen this exam out. Last night, they'd been on his turf and he'd been in control. This morning, the arena was hers.

"Look up," she directed him, and Kent silently obeyed. "Look down." Again, he obeyed, but gripped the arm of the chair tightly. Until that moment, Kent hadn't thought a simple, routine vision exam could be an act of diabolic torture.

Soft music played faintly in the background. The lighting was almost nonexistent. This beautiful blonde was bent over him so closely that he could feel her every breath against his face. Her scent filled his nostrils, and if he moved his hand just a few inches it would be filled with the luscious softness of her breast. Insisting on going through with his exam had definitely been another in the series of mistakes he'd made with this woman. Maybe she had nerves of iron, but he didn't.

"Hmm." Lynda's classic doctor's comment shattered the seductive atmosphere.

"Hmm?" Kent reacted suspiciously. "What does that mean?"

Settling back on her stool, Lynda dropped her ophthalmoscope back into its place, then made a few notations on his record. "Nothing extraordinary," she answered. "Do you do much close work?"

Kent's gaze swept over her. He grinned engagingly. "Not as much as I'd like."

Lynda sent him a killing glare. "So you don't read as much as you'd like?"

"Actually, I do quite a lot of reading."

"Look at the chart on the wall." She handed him a small white plastic paddle. "Cover your left eye and read the smallest line you can with your right."

"No problem. I've always had perfect vision in both eyes," Kent asserted as he easily read the bottom line on the chart.

Lynda made no comment and directed him to repeat the procedure for his left eye. The results were the same, and again when he read the chart with both eyes. "Your distance vision is perfect," she announced.

Kent grinned, triumphantly. "That's what I said. Are we through now?"

"Not quite. Seeing things at a distance isn't all we ask of our eyes." She handed him a card and directed. "Cover your left eye again and read the smallest line you can."

Sure that this was a waste of time, Kent still followed her directive, holding the card at almost arm's length.

Noting the action, Lynda hid her smile and asked him to repeat the procedure with his other eye and then with both.

His action each time was approximately the same. He straightened his arm almost completely as he held the card.

When he'd finished the third reading, she took the card and the paddle from him. While scribbling figures on his record, she purposely emitted another "Hmm..."

"Hmm?" Kent echoed, revealing a touch of irritation.

Lynda ignored his response and asked, "Do you ever experience a burning sensation, tearing or headaches while or after reading for a long period of time?"

"Well...yes," he admitted. "But doesn't everybody after several hours?"

"It can be avoided," was her comment before swinging the phoropter in front of his face.

"Now look here," Kent started, uncomfortably aware of his own defensiveness. He pushed the bulky instrument away from his face.

Lynda promptly swung the phoropter back into position. "No, you look right there," she returned firmly. She spun the dials on the instrument much more rapidly than was necessary except for creating the effect she wanted.

Lenses dropped in and out of place so rapidly, Kent pulled his head back, sure that if he hadn't his lashes would have been caught in the machine. She turned a few more dials, then stood and attached a long rod to the front of the phoropter. A card was attached to the rod and secured at a specific distance. "Look at the letters on the card and tell me which is better, one or two?" Lynda inquired, rapidly changing the lenses before his eyes.

"Eh...two...I think," Kent answered, thinking neither image presented had been particularly good, nor had he been given enough time to form an opinion.

"This one." She gave him a second to focus on the small chart then changed the lens in front of his eyes. "Or this one."

"The first one."

She went on relentlessly, to Kent's way of thinking. All of the powers of the lenses she slid in front of his eyes seemed to blur the letters on the card. Some of them worse than others. Finally, another "Hmm," and she slipped what he prayed was the last set in front of his eyes. "How about this."

Miraculously, everything was clear. "Great," he announced triumphantly, sure that he was looking through nothing but ordinary glass this last time. "So what's the verdict, Doc? Am I a menace on the highways?"

You're a menace all right, she thought. "Nothing about your distance vision to indicate any problems driving...." She purposely let her voice trail off and let the unspoken *but* get the reaction she wanted.

He was squirming, she noted with no small amount of satisfaction. Purposefully, she took her time removing the rod and card from the phoropter before swinging the instrument away. She had a pretty good idea what was going on in his mind.

She wouldn't have made any other patient suffer waiting for her diagnosis, but this was a special case. For far longer than was necessary, she kept her attention directed solely on the exam form, scribbling down three times as many figures as was necessary.

"All right. I can see to drive." Kent's exasperated voice broke the silence. "Give it to me straight. How many months do I have left before I go blind?" he queried, trying for joviality.

Lynda managed not to chuckle. He looked so worried, she almost felt sorry for him. But only almost. "Quite a few months, probably years I should think," she replied, sounding vague.

She spoke slowly, as if she were choosing her words carefully. "I'm going to prescribe corrective lenses for reading and any other time you're using your near vision. As time goes on, we may try some other approaches that will make you as comfortable as possible during the time you have left."

"The time I have left?" All the color drained from Kent's face. "What exactly are you saying?"

Tightening her lips to keep from laughing, Lynda tried for as grim an expression as she could conjure. "I'm saying that you need a little help at near point and most probably will need a little more as the years go on." She could have stopped then, but an imp within her tacked on, "Your age and general good health are on your side, and unless something dramatic happens, I wouldn't think you'd go blind before you're... hmm..."

Kent grew more uncomfortable when Lynda paused, frowning as if she were giving the matter considerable thought. Visions of himself with a white cane and a Seeing Eye dog swirled in his head. He'd adjust, he told himself. There were worse things than blindness. He liked dogs, loved them. How long before one became truly his best friend?

"A hundred and ten," Lynda finished quietly, her tongue in her cheek to maintain a sober expression.

It took a few seconds before the meaning of her words sunk in. Then he began to laugh. "Touché, Doctor." He saluted her successful act of revenge with a nod. "I was going to apologize for any embarrassment I might have caused you last night, but I'd say we're even now. You really had me going," he admitted. "And I thought you were always the consummate professional in the office."

"I am," she confirmed, still maintaining her serious expression though her eyes were dancing. "Come on, I'm going to return you to Jennifer. She's our expert at picking out the perfect frame."

"For whom?" he asked dumbly.

"You."

"But I don't need—"

"Oh, yes, you do, unless you want to continue having headaches or give up reading altogether."

"But—"

"This way, Mr. Berringer." She led him up the hall.

It was the high point of the day for Lynda. She'd managed to put at least a pinprick in this man's ego, and it made her feel good. For the first time since Kent Berringer had started his act the afternoon before, she felt in control of both herself and the world she'd built around her.

After seating Kent in the frame-selection room and instructing him to start trying on anything that appealed to him, Lynda went in search of Jennifer. The reception area was not only vacant but closed down. The cover was on the typewriter. The computer was turned off. The phones had been switched over to the answering machine. It was exactly twelve-thirty, the time the staff was supposed to leave on Saturdays but rarely did. Today was the exception.

"Methinks I smell a rat," Lynda muttered under her breath as she retraced her steps. At least this time she wasn't going to be surprised by Mr. Kent Berringer, alias Slide Hornblower.

"Find anything you like?" she asked as she entered the room.

Kent slid a very expensive frame on his face and glanced at the mirror. "I'll take these," he said as he took the frame off and handed it to Lynda. "How about lunch?"

"There's a good restaurant down the street. Enjoy yourself. That's a designer frame," she stated, trying to convey tactfully that its cost was high. She doubted a musician of only local renown, even one as good as Kent Berringer, made a lot of money. She extracted a similar but far less expensive frame from the board. "Have you tried this one? It's good quality and very similar." As unobtrusively as possible she managed to name the prices of both.

"I like this one better." He stubbornly maintained his preference for the more expensive frame, and Lynda chose not to push the matter any further. She would have had to have been blind not to have noticed that he was wearing expensive shoes, a designer shirt and well-tailored slacks. Maybe local musicians made more money than she thought. Or maybe this one chose to spend most of what he earned on clothes.

Ignoring the charm he oozed with every word and gesture, Lynda carefully maintained a professional distance as she took the necessary measurements. After writing up the order and fee slip, she handed him the top copy of the latter and waited for some reaction to the hefty sum at the bottom.

Kent's only reaction was to inquire, "Would you like full payment today or are you going to bill me?"

"Er—ah—we usually like at least enough to cover the lab costs before we send in the order," she stammered, unable to cover her surprise that he was taking the fee in stride. "You can pay the balance when you come in for your glasses, or we can bill you."

"I'll pay it all today. It'll save us both time and trouble," he said, pulling a checkbook from his pocket and promptly filling out a check for the full amount.

"Thank you," she murmured. She noted the address printed on his check and involuntarily raised an eyebrow. The Waterford Tower, a new condominium high rise overlooking the city and riverfront area. Expensive, exclusive and very fashionable. The man dressed well and lived accordingly. Obviously, he was doing well—at least at the moment.

"We'll call you when your glasses are in. It'll take maybe a week," she explained. With an uncomfortable feeling of déjà vu, she stood and prepared to usher him out of the office.

"Does this restaurant down the street have carry out?" Kent asked as he followed her to the door.

"Yes, they do."

"It's a good day for a picnic, don't you think?"

"I don't know. I haven't been outside since eight o'clock this morning." She'd started to pull the door open when his arm went around her and pushed it closed. "Don't you dare," she warned, ducking beneath his arm and putting several feet between them.

"Dare what?" he asked innocently.

"You know what. Our business is finished. Good day, Mr. Berringer."

"Is it me, or are you always this abrupt with patients?" he asked, leaning his shoulders casually against the door.

Lynda crossed her arms and glared at him. "It's you," she said bluntly, having decided that tact was unnecessary. "I don't like men like you, Mr. Berringer."

"Men like me? Hmm." He pushed away from the door, and Lynda took a step backward. He shook his head slowly as he advanced on her. "It's what you think I am that you think you don't like, Dr. Fisher."

"It's what I know," she corrected quickly, forcing herself to hold her ground.

Stopping with barely an inch left between them, Kent loomed over her. "You know hardly anything at all about me, but you already like what you know."

"No, I don't," Lynda maintained staunchly, managing not to retreat. He was so close, she could feel the heat of his body, almost feel the heavy beat of his heart—or was it her own heart that was thudding so heavily?

"Oh, yes, you do," he said softly, his gaze so penetrating she felt as if he were looking into her soul. "I appeal to a side of you that for some reason you're afraid to acknowledge. Someday I'm going to find out just why."

Lynda swallowed hard, and the tip of her tongue wet her suddenly dry lips. She could feel her body straining toward him, and she fought hard to resist. "You'll never get the chance," she whispered.

"Didn't anyone ever tell you not to say *never*?" he challenged, his voice matching her whisper. He shifted his mesmerizing gaze away from her eyes to her lips. Lynda braced herself not to respond to the kiss she was sure was coming.

It didn't. Kent sent her one more long, lingering look then turned on his heel and promptly left the office. Lynda stared at the closed door, unsure whether she was relieved or disappointed.

She was barely conscious of her fingertips brushing her lips as she let out her pent-up breath and sagged into one of the waiting-room chairs.

Four

Kent whistled as he strolled along the sidewalk. A wicker hamper swung carelessly from one hand. He felt the warmth of the sun on his face and a light breeze ruffling his hair. Overhead was a brilliant blue sky with powder-puff clouds. It was a good day. A perfect day for what he had in mind.

A Jug of Wine, a Loaf of Bread—and Thou
Beside me singing in the Wilderness—

His expression grew rueful. Getting the wine, bread and other foodstuffs had been the easy part. One stop at the gourmet shop up the street from Lynda's office and he'd been able to purchase food, the necessities to serve it with and the hamper to carry everything to a spot along the river where the trees had thick trunks and sweeping boughs and the grass was soft and cool.

Not quite the wilderness, but close enough to set the mood.

Getting the woman to go along with his plans might prove a little more difficult. A simple invitation wasn't going to do it. Lynda Fisher had made it very clear that he was the last man she wanted to spend any time with. So why was he bothering with her?

"Because we have some unfinished business, my dear," he said aloud as he fished in his pocket for his car keys. "Neither one of us has been honest about ourselves, and it's way past time we were."

Clearing up the misconceptions Lynda had about him was only an opening argument for spending any time with her. In the past, there'd been others who'd formed erroneous opinions of him and his character and he'd never bothered to make any real effort to set them straight. He'd always chosen to go about his business and let others find out for themselves what Kent Berringer really stood for. Clearing his good name with Lynda Fisher was the least likely motive for continuing his pursuit of the lovely optometrist, he admitted to himself.

Placing the hamper in the trunk of his car, he ticked off the pros and cons of seeing Lynda Fisher any further. The cons outweighed the pros. Prudence dictated that he get in his car and drive away, forgetting he'd ever met her. Slamming the trunk closed, he chuckled to himself. He decided in favor of the pursuit, despite the odds against success. He'd never been particularly prudent.

Meeting a challenge, now that was his forte. She'd been a challenge since their first confrontation, and less than an hour earlier, she'd literally thrown down the gauntlet. For a man like him, picking it up was irresistible.

A man like him. Maybe total honesty wasn't the best ploy with her, not yet at least. Maybe he'd continue to be little more of what she thought he was and prove his theory that a man like him was exactly what the hidden Lynda Fisher needed in her life.

Grinning, he entered her building. It wasn't until he had his hand on the doorknob of Lynda's office that he felt a faint niggle of doubt that facing a challenge was his only motivation. Ignoring it, he entered and went directly to the receptionist's window. He announced his presence by tapping the desk bell, and saying softly, "Come on out, Dr. Fisher, whomever you are."

Holding his car door open, Kent bowed at the waist. "My lady, my humble little chariot awaits you."

Lynda eyed the flashy red convertible with something akin to shock. She wasn't a sports car expert, but she knew enough to recognize a Ferrari when she saw one. Humble? Hardly. Little? In size, but not price.

There was much more to Kent Berringer than he was letting on. Expensive clothes, expensive condo—and now a car to match. A musician who moonlighted as a stripper couldn't possibly afford such a high standard of living. Or he had other sources of income, sources he was hiding. She should have stuck to her original plan—avoid Kent Berringer completely.

She hesitated. There was still time to call this outing off. She could claim sudden remembrance of a prior commitment or just plain make a dash for the building and lock the doors behind her.

"Here, let me help you. Getting in and out of this baby takes some getting used to." Kent guided her into the car.

Lynda murmured her thanks as she settled herself into the luxuriously upholstered bucket seat. The well-engineered door closed with a quiet finality beside her. The mad dash for escape was out.

Since he hadn't taken no for an answer earlier, she doubted she'd have much success claiming the prior commitment now. Resigning herself, she decided to sit back and enjoy the ride, probably the only time she'd ever sit in something so exotic as a Ferrari.

Running her hands lightly over the butter-soft leather, she could understand the appeal of such a car. To people who had so much money they didn't know what to do with it. And people who spent money when they had it as if a sudden windfall was a sign of continued wealth. People like Papa. . . .

"I should never have let him talk me into this," she told herself as she fumbled with the seat belt. After snapping the safety device in place, she placed her hands primly in her lap.

The man was irresponsible. What she already knew he did to supplement his income as a musician was disreputable. What he did to pay for this car was completely beyond her. He'd embarrassed her—no, humiliated her in public. He'd ruined her birthday celebration. He'd caused her the loss of most of a night's sleep.

And she, Lynda K. Fisher, O.D., found Kent Berringer, musician/stripper, irresistible. Instead of being relieved when the door had closed behind him after his exam, she'd been disappointed! When he'd returned thirty minutes later, she'd actually been glad to see him. If she had any sense at all, she'd ignore his gorgeous blue eyes, devastatingly charming smile and fantastic body, and get right out of his fancy little car.

Kent read the emotions playing across Lynda's features, and elected to say nothing. She was having second thoughts about spending the afternoon with him. He'd bet that if he gave her half a chance, she'd bolt right back into the building and barricade herself in her office.

At the first traffic light, Kent gestured toward the sky. "Look what you would have wasted if you'd stayed cooped up in your office all afternoon."

"All afternoon?" The alarm bells that had been ringing in Lynda's head clanged louder. "I agreed to lunch."

"You agreed to a picnic lunch," Kent corrected. "Whoever heard of a picnic lunch taking less than an afternoon?"

"Lots of people. Responsible people, people with important jobs to do," Lynda replied, hoping that if she were miserable enough company, this ne'er-do-well would turn right around and return her to her office and give up this assault on her. She didn't have time for anyone else in her life, especially this man.

"Important jobs?" Kent drawled.

His expression darkened, and his tone was the hungry lion's growl he'd used twice before. Whatever the consequences, she was going to maintain her stance. Lynda Fisher might have a reputation for being stuffy and staid, but she was no coward.

"Yes, important jobs," she repeated firmly. "Some people are in positions that preclude playing hookey whenever the mood hits. They have to work long and hard for their money."

Kent's chuckle was low and rumbly. She was judging him erroneously again, but it was exactly what he wanted. "And you don't think I know about long hours and hard work?" he challenged smoothly.

"I suppose you do," she said begrudgingly. She guessed he put in some long hours as a musician, and he must have worked hard to get to be as good as he was. But how tough was it to strip off your clothes in public?

For her, it would have been impossible. She would have died first. But not Kent Berringer.

"Look," she began again. "Some people take their responsibilities seriously for they know others are depending on them."

"Maybe too seriously in your case. Don't you ever let yourself play?"

"Play is for children," Lynda dismissed huffily.

"Never for adults?"

"Not if they've truly grown-up," she replied, aware of the bitterness in her tone. She was swept away to another time when she, Suzanne and their mother had suffered because Gerald Fisher had never truly grown up.

Like Kent Berringer, her father had been charming, good looking and had used any excuse to avoid work and responsibility. A beautiful summer day like this day would have provided just such an excuse, and it wouldn't have mattered if taking off would have resulted in a docking of his pay or even the loss of a job.

Pleasure and fun had come first in Gerald Fisher's life. A home for his family, food for their table, clothes for their backs were things that he had assumed would just come no matter what he did. But they hadn't. Money didn't drop from the sky, and there had been too many bad times between the highs when one of Papa's get-rich-quick schemes had actually worked.

Kent decided to let the issue of play drop. He'd pried more than a confession of subterfuge out of his sister. Under cross-examination, Theresa had told him what she knew about Lynda. It wasn't really much, but it was a start and more than enough to pique his already aroused curiosity.

Lynda lived with her divorced younger sister, Suzanne, and Suzanne's two small daughters. Their parents were dead, and Lynda had literally been mother and father to her sister for several years. Supporting herself as well as Suzanne might explain Lynda's workaholic life-style. Yet, Kent sensed there was something more, something painful buried deep within this woman. However, before he delved into her past, there was a problem with the present that had to be cleared up.

"Your sister is a friend of my sister," he stated as he turned onto Riverside Drive. "Did you know?"

"You have a sister?"

The wide-eyed look of incredulity on Lynda's face made him laugh. "Yes, even I have a sister, and a full entourage of family members to boot. Cousins, aunts, uncles, a mother. A pretty respectable bunch, in fact. Theresa and I are the only skeletons in the Berringer family closet. As I recall, you accused me of being just that last evening."

"What has your sister done to warrant that distinction?" she asked, leaving no doubt as to what she thought he did to make him a pariah in his own family.

"My sister is the founder and head of her own company. Theresa's quite the savvy businesswoman."

"And that makes her a skeleton in your family's closet?" Lynda dropped all her stiffness and turned toward Kent as much as the safety belt would allow. "What kind of family do you have that they wouldn't be impressed with such an achievement?"

Kent smiled inwardly. At last she was softening a little, maybe feeling sorry enough for the other radical Berringer that she'd look more kindly on the older one. "A very stiff-necked one, I'm afraid. I told you they were a respectable lot. They don't look too favorably on any family member who deviates from the mold. Very set ideas about everyone's expected role and life-style."

"Is her business successful?"

Kent nodded affirmatively.

"Is it legal?" she asked more slowly. It had suddenly occurred to her that a straitlaced family might have good cause for disapproving of Theresa's business. After all, look what the brother did for a living. Her sympathies were leaning more and more toward the family. She could identify with their feelings; hadn't she suffered countless embarrassments growing up with a reckless father?

"It's legal," he affirmed as he steered his car into a parking space. "I made sure of it."

"*You* made sure of it?"

He unsnapped his seat belt and turned to face her. One arm draped over the steering wheel, the other stretched out across the back of his seat and part of hers, he seemed to fill the car.

"Yes, *I* made sure of it. Believe it or not, I am a law-abiding citizen and enjoy a certain respect in the legal community," he informed her, his voice dropping to the dangerous growl that sent shivers down her spine.

Reason told her she shouldn't believe him, but his steady gaze on hers canceled her reason. Eyes were her business, and she thought she was pretty good at judging character by them. Kent's eyes were too clear, his gaze too steady for him to be lying. She started to ask what he meant by enjoying the respect of the legal community, but he started talking again.

"More importantly—" he leaned closer until her range of vision was filled with nothing but his face and she forgot all about her question; his deep blue eyes held hers captive "—I care about my sister, which brings us to the real reason I brought her up."

"Which is?" She was caught in the mysterious spell he so capably wove over her that her voice came out low. Every breath she took was filled with his scent, and she was drawn forward.

"Which is?" he echoed distractedly. His lips were so close she could feel their warmth. "I did the little blackmailer a favor yesterday."

"Favor?" she murmured just as she closed her eyes.

Kent groaned softly then settled quickly back into his seat. Taking a deep breath, he divulged in rapid syllables, "I am not an employee of Terri's Tributes, but merely agreed to help my sister out in what she claimed was an emergency. She played on my loyalty and caring for her, threw in a little blackmail, suckered me into getting into that ridiculous costume and handed me your address. The rest you know. I muddled through as best I could."

Still recovering from their near kiss, Lynda took several moments to make some sense of his words. She couldn't help the wide smile that spread across her face. "Then you don't moonlight as a stripper?"

"Uh-uh." Kent shook his head. "Believe me, yesterday marked both my debut and my final performance as a stripper."

"Oh, thank God," Lynda said in obvious relief.

He grinned. "Was I that bad?"

"No, you were really very good," she assured quickly. When she saw the devilish twinkle in his eyes, she began to stammer. "I mean...I suppose you were...you're certainly attractive enough for the job...and you...you're really not a stripper?"

"No, I'm not," he stated very firmly. "Your reputation won't suffer by being seen with me. I really am quite respectable."

"You do more than play trombone with a jazz ensemble?" The moment the question was out Lynda realized how much it sounded like a put-down. She'd implied that being a jazz musician, no matter how good he was, wasn't respectable. The teasing smile had vanished from his face. "I'm sorry," she apologized. "I didn't mean that the way it sounded."

"It's okay," he said, but his tone indicated just the opposite. "I've heard it before. Actually, I do do other things, but we'll get into all that some other time. Right now, there are a few more details you should know about yesterday.

"My sister is a friend of your sister Suzanne," he reminded. "Now do you understand why Theresa suddenly needed her big brother as a stand-in for her alleged ailing stripper?"

"We were set up," Lynda said, stating the obvious. "Why, that little—I thought it was her. Boy, she was a good actress last night. When I get my hands on her, I'm going to, to—''

''Let's eat lunch.'' Kent slid out of the car and helped Lynda. He suggested with a grin, ''Plotting vengeance is always better on a full stomach. Besides, you should have all the facts before you exact some sort of retribution. I'll fill you in on all the details while we eat.''

Kent extracted the picnic hamper and a blanket, which he laid out by the riverbank.

Watching him uncork a bottle of wine, Lynda asked, ''How did your sister get you to do it?''

After filling their glasses, Kent thrust the wine bottle back into the bucket of ice. ''The element of surprise,'' he said truthfully. Leaving out his stint in Chippendale's band, he told Lynda about the miraculous recovery of the college student and how it had led to a full confession from his sister.

''Our sisters met when Theresa took her dog to the veterinarian that Suzanne works for. Since old Buff was having some foot problems that required frequent treatment, Theresa and Suzanne got to be friends,'' he explained, emptying the hamper. He handed Lynda a plate heaped with gourmet delights.

''Suzanne evidently wanted to do something really special for your birthday, and that's Theresa's business. Instead of a bouquet of balloons, a huge cake or any of the other more tasteful offerings on Theresa's list of salutations, they went for the stripper and most specifically me as the performer to assure that we'd meet.''

Lynda snorted her disapproval as she bit into the filled croissant he'd handed her. ''There are other more conventional ways of introducing people.''

"Would you have agreed to any of them?"

Lynda shrugged. "Probably not. I really don't have time to waste on a miserable evening with somebody else's idea of the perfect man for me. How about you?"

"Same. I probably would have tried my damnedest to avoid it. My guess is that our sisters both know that."

"And so they resorted to something so dramatic neither of us knew what was happening."

"Looks that way."

"And last night at Trafalgar Square? Was that part of the deal, too?"

Kent winced. He couldn't place the blame for what had happened last evening on anyone but himself. "You're not referring to the coincidence of our being at the same place and then being introduced by Jay, are you?" Lynda's frosty glare was his answer. "Thought not."

If the top button of Kent's polo shirt hadn't already been unbuttoned, he would have undone it right now. He was definitely feeling very uncomfortable.

Lynda watched him closely. "Why." It wasn't a question.

Kent didn't miss the firm demand in her husky voice. She wanted a full explanation accompanied by an apology. His conscience had already told him that she deserved both.

"My behavior was inexcusable, and I sincerely apologize." Extending his hand, palm up, in a gesture of peace, he asked, "Can we start over?"

Lynda eyed his hand warily. "Are you apologizing for everything?"

He sent her a thousand-watt smile. "Everything but kissing you," he told her unabashedly, his eyes full of merriment.

Lynda gave him a long look before relenting. In all honesty, she wasn't really sorry about those kisses, either. Embarrassed by them, maybe a little frightened, but not sorry.

"Apology accepted." She placed her hand on his and wasn't surprised when he wrapped his fingers around her slender palm. Nor was she surprised by the feeling of warmth that invaded her as a result of his touch. All he had to do was look at her and she felt as if she were in a sauna.

Intellectually, he was all wrong for her. His not being a stripper made no difference, nor did his claim that he was respectable. He was too frivolous and had all the trappings of a playboy. He wasn't her type, but she couldn't deny that a chemistry existed between them that drew her as strongly as a flame drew a moth. With disastrous results, she reminded herself, and immediately stiffened.

His gaze steady, he ignored her slight sign of resistance. He brought her hand slowly to his mouth and placed a soft kiss on it. When he turned it over and pressed a lingering kiss on her palm, she didn't care that she chanced burning in the flame.

"Thank you. I behaved like such a jackass, I really didn't expect you to forgive me," he admitted, still holding her hand as well as her gaze. For a long moment, it was as if they were truly alone. She wasn't aware of anything but Kent, the man with the bluest eyes and most enchanting smile.

The roar of a motorboat finally shattered the enchantment. Kent let go of her hand and reached for the wine bottle. "There's a little more wine. Let's have a toast."

Without waiting for her permission, he filled both glasses. Raising his, he offered, "To us. A new beginning." He tapped the rim of his glass on Lynda's.

Lynda took a sip. The crisp flavor of the Chablis jolted her taste buds and switched her reason back to full power. Abruptly, she set the glass down.

"Something wrong?" Kent inquired.

"No. I mean yes. Well, not really." She halted, then started over. It was her turn for a confession. "I swore off champagne only this morning, and here I am on my third glass of wine and it's only—" She glanced at her watch. "Good heavens, it's almost three o'clock."

"A lovely time of day, don't you think?" Stretching his body out on the blanket, Kent propped his head on one arm and balanced his glass on his chest. He swirled the wine. "No bubbles. It's not champagne, so your vow is still unbroken."

"Wine is wine. Bubbles or no bubbles, the effect's the same," Lynda muttered as she reached for the shoes she'd so carelessly kicked off. She quickly put them on and started gathering up the remains of their picnic.

"Just what are you doing?" Kent inquired.

"Isn't it obvious?" she answered, snapping lids on Styrofoam containers and stuffing trash in a plastic bag. "I need to get back to my office, and the quicker we clear up, the quicker we can be away from here."

"But we haven't had dessert."

"I don't need any dessert, and besides you must have forgotten it."

"How does hazelnut *gelato* sound?"

Her favorite. How could he know that? Probably just a coincidence that it was his favorite, too. She almost licked her lips in anticipation then shook her head. "Sounds wonderful, but I don't see any freezer here and I prefer my *gelato* frozen," she quipped as she settled the last of the leftovers into the hamper. "Okay, we're all ready to go."

To Lynda's relief, Kent sat up and reached for the hamper. The relief was only short lived for he merely set it back down—off the blanket this time—handed her her still-full wineglass, then lay down again. "Relax, kick your shoes off and enjoy the sunshine," he instructed and closed his eyes. "The concert doesn't begin for several more hours. We'll have plenty of time to pick up the *gelati* from a vendor when we meander on down to the amphitheater."

"A concert? Tonight? But I can't possibly spend all day here and go to a concert tonight," Lynda argued.

Kent opened one eye, gave her a once-over look, then closed it. "There's no need to worry about changing," he said drowsily. "It's pretty casual. You look terrific. That skirt and blouse you're wearing are perfect."

"But I—"

"Like art and music?"

"Well, yes, but—"

"We're in luck. Today's the first day of the Riverfront Art Festival, and the symphony's playing at the amphitheater tonight."

"But I—"

"Need a nap as much as I do. You've got smudges under your pretty eyes, Dr. Fisher." He stretched out one arm. "Here you can put your head on my shoulder. I've been told it's pretty comfortable."

Five

Open-air concerts on star-studded summer nights could be magic, if the listener weren't having so much difficulty finding a comfortable position on a blanket spread out on the grassy ground.

With her legs stretched out before her, one arm propping her upright, Lynda tried to ignore the strain in her back and the creeping numbness in the hand that was supporting most of her weight. Arching her back, she flexed her shoulders slightly to relieve the strain.

"You can use my shoulder again."

Lynda's inner caution screamed a warning against the tantalizing offer. She knew just how comfortable Kent Berringer's shoulder was. She'd snoozed away the afternoon with her head on it.

When she hadn't been able to roust Kent from his comfortable position on the blanket that afternoon, she'd contemplated walking to the nearest phone booth and calling her sister to come rescue her. After a couple more sips of wine, she'd rejected the idea. A phone booth had been nowhere in sight. Even if one had been, she hadn't felt like answering any questions about the whys and hows that had led to her having a picnic with Kent Berringer. Suzanne would have believed that her matchmaking was working, which it wasn't! Not by a long shot. Lynda didn't like this man one whit. She was attracted to him, yes, but she didn't like him, and today was going to mark the end of their association.

She'd sat there glaring daggers at the man sleeping so blissfully while she alternately rehearsed lectures for her sister and fortified her conviction that Kent Berringer was all wrong for her. In the absence of anything else to do, she drank the rest of her wine and then, stifling yawns, began to consider lying down just for a few minutes. But she'd had no intentions of taking Kent up on his offer to use his shoulder as a pillow. She'd carefully placed herself on the farthermost edge of the blanket—to rest, not to sleep.

The next thing she'd known was the butterfly-light brush of Kent's lips against her forehead. She'd struggled into wakefulness and found herself in his arms, looking up into those wonderful blue eyes.

"Good evening," he'd said, flashing her a broad smile that was guaranteed to melt the coldest heart. "Feel better?"

She had felt better, but she'd felt compelled to cling to some annoyance with him for causing her to waste valuable working hours. However, by the time they'd strolled through the art show and eaten a variety of delicacies from the booths tucked between the artists' displays, her work had slipped from its place of prominence in her mind and she'd found she was thoroughly enjoying herself. It had felt good to be carefree and walk hand in hand with a good-looking man who was also delightful company.

Leaning on his shoulder again would be delightful, too, and far more comfortable, even sensible. Why risk back sprain? She shifted the few inches necessary to bring herself in contact with him. "That's the second sensible thing you've done all day," he whispered into her ear.

"I haven't done anything sensible all day," she whispered back.

"Exactly," he agreed, shifting his legs and settling her between them. He gently pushed her head against his shoulder, then curled both arms around her waist. "The first sensible thing you did was to take off with me for the day."

"You call that sensible?"

"R and R, sweetheart. A little rest and relaxation never hurt anybody. In fact, it's been proven that it has just the opposite effect. Actually improves productivity."

"You think so, huh?" she challenged teasingly, liking the feel of his steady heartbeat against her back and the security of being held by strong arms. It felt good to lean on someone else for a change, to depend on someone other than herself. When she realized where her thoughts were going, she reminded herself that her position was purely a temporary, practical measure. His body was nothing more than a substitute for a chair.

"I know so," he mumbled, nuzzling her temple. "I'm an authority on it."

"R and R or productivity?" Her breath caught in her throat when Kent moved his lips down the side of her face. Unable to stop herself, she squirmed in reaction to the sensation that jolted through her body when he touched the tip of his tongue to her earlobe.

"Both," he told her as he nibbled his way around the edge of her ear.

Desperate to escape the sweet havoc he was wreaking on her defenses, she turned her head. But, in her disoriented state, she turned toward him rather than away. Her gaze was caught by his; the intent in his clear. Their lips were a fraction apart. "Oh, please," she begged. Whether she was begging him not to take advantage of their proximity or begging him to kiss her, she wasn't sure herself.

"Lynda," he sighed against her lips before covering them with his. Firm and warm, they enticed and inflamed her senses. Just as the dormant fires within her were springing to life, Kent lifted his mouth from hers.

Lynda moaned softly in protest. Pressing a finger against her throbbing lips, he promised, "Later. Kissing you is dangerous, lady. Even I will go only so far in public."

Kent's statement brought Lynda sharply back to reality. All too clearly, she remembered where they were. Mortified that she'd so easily abandoned all sense of propriety, she wanted nothing so much as to be far away from Kent Berringer. Though his disclosures at lunch had relieved some of her concerns about his character, he still epitomized all she didn't want or admire in a man. Around him, she might be like a moth drawn to the flame, but he was as indolent as the grasshopper in Aesop's fable, and she far preferred the industrious ant.

She'd enjoyed his company this afternoon, but she didn't want a steady diet of it. And she didn't want to have any more disturbing memories of him that would keep her awake at night. She tried to move out of his arms, but he tightened them at her waist.

"Stay exactly where you are," he growled in her ear. "Relax and enjoy the music. Stop being so afraid of what's happening between us."

"Nothing's happening between us," Lynda returned with gritted teeth, doubting the statement the moment she made it.

His answer was a hushed laughter, and she felt every ripple in his chest. "If that kiss was nothing, I can't wait for whatever you call something."

"You're going to wait a long time," she stated as firmly as she was able. It was impossible to deny that she and Kent were an explosive combination. Explosives were dangerous, but they could be controlled. She only had to keep herself out of his company, and she was determined to do just that—starting tomorrow.

For what little was left of today, she was resigned to flirt with danger. Reclining in Kent's arms for the remainder of the concert was as close to danger that Lynda was going to chance.

The concert was drawing to a close, and Lynda settled back to enjoy it, secure in the knowledge that she was once again in control of her life. Today, when she'd let Kent take over her day, had been a momentary lapse.

Maybe Kent was right and she'd needed R and R. It had been pleasant. She did feel rested, and the music was relaxing, even if she couldn't say the same for the man holding her. Every nerve in her body was on alert to him. Under no circumstances was she going to be foolish enough to allow a repeat of the kiss they had shared moments before.

Ravel was the final composer on the program. His music, like that of the others on the program, appealed to the senses, and Lynda was not immune to its hypnotism. Closing her eyes, she let the music flow through her. Her body swayed with the stirring rhythm.

Lynda's movement didn't go unnoticed by Kent. If he'd needed one last piece of evidence to prove his theory about her, he had it. The way she'd responded to his kisses and now her response to the music told him he was holding the most sensuous woman he'd ever known. It took every bit of willpower he had to keep from groaning aloud with each brush of her body against his.

It wasn't until the music grew louder that Lynda realized what was happening. Reclining in Kent's arms and answering the energy of the music was flirting too close to the flame.

She quickly extricated herself from Kent. "Would you mind leaving now?" She gathered up her purse, indicating she wasn't actually asking. "It's already late, and I'd like to avoid being caught in a traffic jam getting out of here," she said as an excuse.

Kent was only too happy to accommodate her. He was having trouble enough refraining from embarrassing them both. With an economy of motion and noise, so as not to disturb the other concertgoers, he gathered the blanket and hamper, and followed Lynda.

Little was said as they made their way to the parking lot. They exchanged a few mundane pleasantries during the drive back to Lynda's office, but spent most of the time alone with their thoughts. Kent ruled the day a perfect beginning. He was positive Lynda had enjoyed it as much as he. Thus, to an imaginary judge, he offered another piece of evidence for his case that the man he'd so far presented to Lynda was exactly what she needed.

When they pulled up beside the lone car, a small economy compact, parked behind her building, Kent anticipated an exceedingly gratifying embrace that would further his case even though he noted Lynda already had her keys in one hand and her other on the door handle.

"Thank you for a lovely day," she offered the second Kent had pulled his car to a complete stop. She was out of the car and closing the door by the time Kent got to her side.

"I always escort a lady home," he explained as he took her arm. "Or in this case, to her car."

"That's hardly necessary."

"Maybe not, but my mother tried to make a gentleman of me."

"Are you saying she didn't entirely succeed?" Lynda teased, unlocking her car.

"Enough to make me realize that some of what she was trying to get across would definitely put me in an advantage in given situations."

"Such as?" she asked, stepping out of the way as she swung her car door open. The action put her squarely into Kent's open arms.

"This," he said as he closed his arms around her and brought his mouth down on hers, silencing any protest she might have made.

Somewhere in the back of Lynda's mind a protest formed, but the entrancement of his tongue tracing the outline of her lips superseded all thought. His light touch unleashed a feminine hunger she couldn't deny. She opened to his entreaty and mewed softly when his tongue slipped between her parted lips. Whether the sound was protest or delight, she couldn't have said.

The tender exploration of his tongue inside her mouth was drugging, dulling her every thought except one—desire. She wasn't a passive participant. Recklessly, she wrapped her arms around his neck. With only the slightest coaxing from him, she slid her tongue into his mouth, tasting, teasing, exciting, giving as much as she received.

With a groan of male satisfaction, Kent molded Lynda to his body. Feeling the lush press of her breasts against his chest and the softness of her belly against his hardened groin was a torment that set off an overpowering need to be inside her.

"Oh, God!" Kent groaned, wrenching his mouth away from temptation. When he brought his breathing under enough control to talk, he said, "I'd say that was something, wouldn't you?" Shaking, he set her slightly away from him. "Lie if you have to, but tell me you don't go up like a volcano everytime a man kisses you."

Lynda wrenched totally out of his grasp. The passion that had glazed her eyes a moment before fled. A wounded look replaced it, and Kent wanted to call back his words. He hadn't been thinking straight, still wasn't. "Lynda, I—"

"Think what you like, Mr. Berringer," she said coldly. "Goodbye!" She got into her car, slamming and locking the door. Ignoring the tapping on her window and the muffled words coming through the glass, she inserted the key into the ignition. Some luck remained with her this day; the little car sprang to life. Quickly she threw it into gear and drove off.

Through tear-filled eyes, Lynda steered toward her house, alternately condemning Kent and herself with each block. What on earth happened to her whenever he kissed her? She didn't even like the man.

She turned onto her quiet street lined with modest houses and went past the cream-colored one with the blue shutters that sheltered her little family. It wasn't midnight yet and Suzanne might still be awake. Lynda was in no mood to face her sister.

Heading toward the outerbelt, she began to circle the city. Two hours later, she felt it safe to return home. She laughed in self-derision as she pulled to a stop in her driveway. Good old Lynda Fisher, the serious student, the even more serious professional, the woman who'd reached the grand old age of thirty with so few men in her life she could count them on one hand, turned into a wild woman every time Kent Berringer kissed her.

"Who'd believe it?" she asked aloud as she got out of her car. Certainly none of the other males who'd attempted to get close to her over the years. Prude, cold, ice maiden. Those had been some of the kinder terms that had been hurled at her.

It wasn't that she was totally against men or the idea of ever marrying one. She merely had far more pressing and important things to do than dating. Those few dates she had had in high school and college had been

disappointing. The boys and later the men had sometimes seemed interesting companions, but anything
beyond conversation had been a turn-off.

"Kissing Kent Berringer is no turn-off," she muttered as she let herself in the back door. The driving
hadn't relaxed her or in any way dimmed the effects of
the final embrace she'd shared with Kent. Just thinking about being held in his arms, being kissed so mas-
terfully, caused a soft moan to sound from her throat
and her knees to go weak.

The house was quiet, indicating that everyone, including her sister, was in bed. The house was also
dark, but for the light over the kitchen range and another low one in the hallway. She tiptoed to her bedroom, making as little noise as possible. Tomorrow
morning would come all too soon, and there would be
no escape from Suzanne's inquisition.

Stripping off her clothes, Lynda climbed into bed.
Sleep came no more easily than it had the night before. Her body tingled in remembrance of being
pressed against Kent's, and her cheeks burned with the
humiliation of his accusation.

The night before she'd tossed and turned. This
night, she curled into a tight ball and let the tears she'd
fought for hours finally fall freely.

"More French toast!" Moe demanded.

"Have to say the magic word, Moe," prompted
Arrie, full of the righteousness of being the older sister by an entire year.

"Please, Aunt Lyndy?"

Lynda smiled at the dimpled little face. "Coming
right up, baby," she responded as she scooped the last
slice of toast from the pan and placed it on the plat-

ter. She'd taken over the end of breakfast while Suzanne took her turn in the shower. With only one bathroom to meet the needs of two grown females and two small ones, efficiency was a necessity on Sunday mornings when all four of them were on the same schedule.

"I'm not a baby!" Maureen announced, her elfin features set in a belligerent frown. "I'm a big girl. I go to school just like Arrie."

"Not real school." Ariel giggled. "You're still going to be at Little People Day Care, that's a baby school. I'm going to Windemere School," she announced, naming the elementary school located just up the street.

"You're just a kindygarter. That's a baby at the big school," Maureen fired back defensively.

"I'm not a baby! You are!"

"Am not!"

"Are to!"

"Girls!" Lynda interrupted her nieces before the argument went any further. Force of habit had prompted her to call Maureen baby. She made a mental note to refrain from doing it again, at least when Ariel was around. "Neither one of you are babies. You're both grown up young ladies who better get a move on or we'll all be late for church."

Their egos soothed, the two dove back into their breakfast with gusto while the peacemaker picked at hers. Her eyes felt gritty, her head ached dully and her body felt shaky. She could have used several more hours in bed, but her internal clock had awakened her at the regular time as effectively as any alarm clock.

Even if she had been able to convince her body to go back to sleep, her conscience would've kept her awake.

She and Suzanne were as strong in their belief that children learned best by example as they were in their conviction that the girls should attend Sunday school regularly. Not attending services themselves would have been hypocritical in their minds.

She stared down at her plate. Her favorite breakfast held little appeal. Her thoughts, no matter how much she wanted them elsewhere, kept drifting to the man who'd caused her miserable night. She munched absently on a strip of bacon and reached blindly for her coffee mug, tuning out the children's chatter until she heard, "We ever goin' to have more babies at our house?"

"You have to have a daddy to make babies, dummy," Arrie answered her sister. "We only have mommys at this house."

"Aunt Lyndy's not a mommy," Moe returned with authority. "She's an op . . . op—what are you, Aunt Lyndy?"

"I'm an optometrist, darling. That's an eye doctor."

"Can you be an op...optom-trist and a mommy?"

"Yes, I could," Lynda told her niece matter-of-factly. Crossing her fingers that this line of conversation was at an end, she stood and started clearing the table.

"Do you wanna be a mommy?" Moe asked.

Lynda placed the plates in the sink and started running water over them. "Someday."

"Any time soon?" Suzanne asked from the doorway.

"No," Lynda drawled, sending her sister a pointed glare that she hoped would convince Suzanne to drop the subject. Feeling a pat on her thigh, she looked down at Moe, surprised to see such a serious expression on the usual pixie face.

"Don't be sad, Aunt Lyndy. Arrie and me'll help you find a daddy so you can have babies."

"Eh...thank you, sweetheart, but that won't be necessary."

"And why not?" Suzanne asked, a teasing light shining in her eyes, the dimples in her cheeks flashing mischievously. "Could it be you've already found one?"

"It could be that some people ought to keep their noses out of other people's business," Lynda stated firmly, preparing a washcloth for the after-breakfast cleanup. "Come on, girls, let's get the syrup cleaned off and get going. Sunday school starts in less than a half hour." Over her nieces' heads, she sent her sister a quelling glare. "You I'll deal with later."

Six

—————

"Oh, come on, Lynda," Suzanne prodded good naturedly hours later. "Admit it, you had a good time yesterday."

Up to her elbows in dishwater, Lynda contemplated scooping up a handful of the suds and flipping it in her sister's face—anything to wipe the smug look off. Instead, she directed her energy toward scrubbing the last pan used in making their traditional Sunday pot roast. If only she hadn't felt compelled to call Suzanne the evening before and explain why she wouldn't be coming home for dinner, she wouldn't have set herself up for this inquisition. Her sister had had too many hours to give her imagination free rein.

"You were with that gorgeous man all day," Suzanne reminded her. "You must have been enjoying yourself or you would have been home a lot sooner than 2:00 a.m."

Totally exasperated, Lynda considered screaming, but emotional displays weren't her way of dealing with things. However, she hadn't been dealing with anything in the last couple of days in her usual, practical manner. She was beginning to feel like a stranger to herself. In the course of forty-eight hours, she'd gone from a woman in total charge of her life to one with a will about as stiff as a wet noodle.

This conversation was a perfect example. It wasn't going at all as she'd planned. As soon as Moe and Arrie had gone out to play, Lynda had been determined to take the offensive and let her sister know in no uncertain terms exactly what she thought of both her present and her past attempt at matchmaking. Instead, it had been Suzanne who'd gone on the offensive, insisting that Lynda tell her every detail of the previous day and evening.

"Okay, I had a good time, but that's all there was to it," Lynda said. "We had a picnic, took in the art show and then the concert. I doubt I'll ever see him again." She hoped that her statement would turn out true.

Suzanne stopped drying the roasting pan and gaped at her sister. "You stayed out until the wee hours with the man who kissed you the night before as if there were no tomorrow and you claim you're never going to see him again? What is the matter with you?"

"Absolutely nothing!" Lynda snapped, her temper flaring. "Which is why I don't need any help from you in finding a man. Maybe I'm just not interested, or maybe I can spend some time with someone and have it be nothing more than it was—a pleasant, relaxing escape from the office."

"Oh, sure, an escape from your office." Suzanne snorted. "What'd he do? Show up after the last patient yesterday morning, grab you by the hair and drag you out of that salt mine?"

"It's not a salt mine. I love my work."

"That's about all you love," Suzanne muttered disgustedly as she hung up the dish towel.

"That is not true and you know it." Lynda grabbed the towel Suzanne had just hung up. Her jerky movements as she dried her hands indicated her distress.

"Oh, Lynda, I am sorry," Suzanne apologized, her sincerity clear by the penitent expression in her eyes. "That was unfair of me. I know you love me and the girls, but you spend so many hours at the office, you have little time for anything else. It wasn't so bad before Dr. Kelsey had the heart attack, but since then, we almost never see you. That practice is too big for one person. Dr. Kelsey knew that when he took you on as an associate. Have you considered getting another O.D. to help out until Dr. Kelsey is back?"

"I've thought about it," Lynda admitted, folding and refolding the towel. "But all the extra money I'm earning right now has already paid off the last of my education loans, and for the first time I can ever remember, the Fisher family has a savings account with some real money in it."

Leaning against the kitchen counter, Suzanne shook her head at her sister. "I understand how important all that is, but I really think you should slow down a bit. I worry about you waking up someday and realizing you've let life pass you by."

"And so you decided to put a little life in my life?" Lynda queried sarcastically. She folded her arms and leaned against the counter. "Did it ever occur to you that I might just be perfectly happy with my life?"

"Are you?"

"Yes, I am." Or at least I was until you meddled in it, she added silently. "I have you and the girls. A career I really love." She paused and looked around the kitchen of the little house she'd so proudly put a down payment on after her first year in practice. "And this house," she continued. "My life is full. I don't need anything else in it."

"What if you didn't have me and the girls?"

Suzanne's question struck Lynda forcefully. She'd taken care of her sister so long that she couldn't imagine not continuing to do so. It had started when Mama had died. She'd been twelve and Suzanne only six. They'd still had Papa for eight more years, but in many ways he'd been more child than parent, and so Lynda had essentially taken over the rearing of her little sister.

"What are you saying?" Lynda asked once she'd recovered from the shock of the question. "Why wouldn't you and the girls be here living with me?"

In a very quiet voice, Suzanne reminded, "I'm graduating at the end of fall quarter, Lynda. As a certified veterinary technician, I'll be earning more, and as soon as I can, I want to get a place of my own."

"But this is your home," Lynda maintained stubbornly.

Just as stubbornly, Suzanne returned, "No, this is your home. You've been wonderful, and I couldn't have made it without you, but I need to stand on my own two feet."

Gauging the look on Suzanne's face, Lynda knew she had a battle on her hands.

"Look, Lynda. I'm twenty-four years old. I have two children. I'll always be grateful that you took us in after Rick left me, but I can't sponge off my big sister forever."

"You haven't been sponging off me." The words nearly exploded out of Lynda's mouth. "We're family! Families support each other and live together."

"Yes, they do. But adult children have to make their own nests."

"When they're ready. You're not ready!"

"Not yet, but soon I will be."

The doorbell chimed just as the back door opened. Moe and Arrie tumbled into the kitchen, requesting cool drinks. While Suzanne saw to her daughters' needs, Lynda headed for the front door.

Still smarting from the argument, Lynda didn't bother to check to see who was waiting outside, but flung the door wide open. Kent Berringer stood as bold as brass on her doorstep. Lynda considered flinging the door shut in his face, but Kent wasn't alone.

A young woman, who bore a striking resemblance to Kent, stood just behind him. She had to be his sister. And by the way she was fidgeting, she was feeling very uneasy.

Unable to think of anything remotely appropriate to say by way of greeting, Lynda continued to stare at the callers. Finally, Kent took the initiative and provided the introductions. "I thought it only appropriate that you meet the other person responsible for making your birthday so memorable."

With a firm grip on his sister's elbow, he guided her over the threshold. To Lynda, he remarked sarcastically, "I'm sure you'd just love to thank my sister for the birthday present she sent you."

Lynda's eyes were shooting daggers, but not at Theresa. When she finally found her voice its tone was dripping even more sarcasm. "Given the opinion you seem to have of me, I suppose it's only natural that you would assume I wouldn't be so polite as to thank someone for a birthday present." Turning to Theresa, she forced a smile. "Thank you, Theresa. The present was . . . eh . . . interesting."

"Aunt Lyndy, didn't you know what the present was?" came a loud whisper from the vicinity of Lynda's knees. She looked down to see a wide-eyed Moe staring solemnly up at her.

"Yes, I did, sweetheart," Lynda answered, hoping that the subject was closed.

"Then why'd you say it was interesting?" The towheaded four-year-old's words were meant only for her aunt, but had the strength and volume of a stage whisper. "That's what Mommy says about my pictures when she doesn't know what they are."

"I know, but I did know what the present was," Lynda assured her niece. Out of the corner of her eye, she caught the mischievous gleam spreading on Kent's face. She damned the fates that had sent Moe into the foyer at such an inopportune moment and the fact that she'd used the word *interesting* to describe the present. Obviously Kent was too pleased with her choice of word.

Moe's little face was conveying confusion, and Lynda knew she'd better come up with some fast explaining to stop the questions threatening to spill from that grape-juice-mustachioed mouth. "Grown-ups sometimes use the word *interesting* because something was just that. Interesting.''

"Real interesting?" Kent queried, looking even more pleased with himself.

Lynda refused to dignify his question with an answer, and the glare she sent him told him so.

"Where's the present? Can I see it?" Moe asked innocently, and Lynda could think of no response except a series of idiotic stammerings and repetitions of the word *present*.

Suzanne and Arrie made their entrance, and the five-year-old promptly echoed her sister's sentiments. Lynda looked to her sister for assistance then decided she had the perfect opportunity for retribution. "Suzanne, explain to your daughters what you and your friend gave me for my birthday."

Suzanne began with an almost perfect repetition of Lynda's stammerings. Her two daughters were far too sharp to be put off with nonsense, and in the end Suzanne was forced to admit that Kent was the present.

"That man?" Arrie pointed her pudgy finger at Kent. Kent lost some of his aplomb at the disdain in the little girl's voice, and Lynda wanted to applaud.

"A person can't be a present," Moe added with finality. "You can't put a person in a box and wrap them up, so that's not a present."

"Unwrapping a present is the best part of getting a present," Kent interjected. His statement earned vigorous agreement from the two little girls. "Aunt Lyndy didn't get to unwrap me, I unwrapped myself, but it was still fun, wasn't it, Aunt Lyndy?"

Lynda gulped her shock and turned quickly to her sister. "Weren't you going to take the girls to the zoo today?" Didn't that man have any sense? Even his sister, the woman in the business of providing strippers for events, seemed to understand that the conversation was venturing into deep water; she was sending her brother frantic eye signals.

Suzanne jumped on Lynda's reminder as if it were a life raft. "Come on, girls, let's get the juice off your faces and our comfortable shoes on." She was halfway down the hall to the bathroom when she called over her shoulder, "Theresa? How about it? Want to spend the day at the zoo?"

"I'd love it! Let me help you with the girls." Theresa exited so quickly it was almost as if she evaporated.

Left alone, Lynda and Kent stood in silence. She was bristling, and her silence should have been as effective as a loud scream. It wasn't. He leaned nonchalantly against the wall as if totally unaware of her growing rage.

Kent was enjoying the new image of the very proper Dr. Lynda Fisher far too much to be distracted by her obvious displeasure with him. She was wearing short, faded cutoffs and a sleeveless T-shirt. Her hair was in a pony tail, and fine wisps curled around her face and at her nape. She looked terrific.

Her legs were every bit as long and beautifully shaped as he'd imagined, and he let his gaze roam slowly up from her slender ankles to her smooth thighs. Her breasts were high and full beneath the snug fit of the knit fabric. His gaze reached her face, and his enjoyment came to a sudden halt.

The only word to do justice to her expression was *thunderous*.

"You're not thrilled to see me today, are you?" They both knew it was a statement of fact and treated it as such. Lynda merely pointed to the still-open door.

Daunted but not ready to surrender, Kent tried a different tack, humility with a touch of honesty. "What I said last night was way out of line and I apologize. My only excuse for making such an asinine remark is that I was in shock. My reaction to kissing you, holding you, isn't exactly mild and I'm having a tough time dealing with it."

Though inwardly she felt a thrill of satisfaction that she'd had the same effect on him as he'd had on her, Lynda refused to be appeased. "Then I suggest you choose a sensible solution to this problem. Avoidance."

Kent shook his head slowly. "No way. I'm surprised by what happens between us, but I'm not scared of it."

"And you think I am?"

"Aren't you?"

"Absolutely not!" Her response was a lie and she knew it; she was scared to death of the volatile chemistry between herself and Kent. Given free rein, she was sure any relationship between them would lead to total heartbreak on her part. Being so attracted to someone meant destruction!

"Prove it. Spend today with me," he invited, flashing her that charming grin.

"I can't," she declared, though she felt a trap closing in on her. "I have things to do that can't be put off."

"Like what? Not more paperwork at your office, I hope. This is Sunday. Surely even you take one day off a week."

His challenge reopened the wound from Suzanne's earlier accusation that Lynda loved only her work. She flinched. Did everyone see her as that single-minded? So one-dimensional? Thank goodness she did have other things to do this day that took precedence over the patient records forming a mountain on her desk at the office.

With no small amount of smugness, she enumerated, "I have a lawn that needs to be mowed, a hedge that needs trimming and a down spout that needs to be reattached. Those are at the top of the list. Do you want the full rundown or is that enough to convince you that I have responsibilities and can't afford to waste another day playing around?"

Kent scanned the yard. "The grass isn't too high and the hedge is still pretty presentable. Looks as if they could wait another day or two."

"Neither Suzanne nor I will have any time until next weekend to get at the yard. By then, we'd need a hay-bailer to deal with the grass." As she'd done what seemed like thousands of times to her in her dealings with this man, she grasped the knob in anticipation of closing the door on Kent Berringer's back.

"Now, you run along and find another little play-mate," she directed condescendingly, purposely sounding as if she were dealing with a juvenile. For that was exactly how she was beginning to think of him. He had a fully mature man's body, but his emotional growth was definitely far behind in development. Despite what he might assert, she did know what kind of man he was.

Kent wasn't about to give up this battle and fired another volley. "But you're letting your sister go off and play for the rest of the day."

Her fists clenched, her teeth clamped together, Lynda faced him. "It's really none of your business, but Suzanne had the lawn chores last weekend and she promised this zoo trip to the girls all week. Nothing short of a disaster would make her break that promise. It's called commitment to something, someone, other than yourself."

Suddenly exhausted, she sighed in exasperation and sagged against the door. "Oh, why do I bother? Someone like you couldn't possibly understand. Just go."

"For your information I do understand something about commitment."

"We're on our way," Suzanne said, sweeping in with her daughters and Theresa, effectively cutting off anything further Kent might have said. "Kiss Aunt Lyndy goodbye and say goodbye to Mr. Berringer, girls."

While the farewells were being made, Kent had a chance to assess Lynda and the surroundings. She looked so tired, it was all he could do to keep from scooping her up in his arms, laying her down on the living room sofa and spending the rest of the day waiting on her every whim.

He was sure she hadn't gotten any more sleep than he had the night before, but he didn't think that was all that accounted for her apparent exhaustion. If what he guessed was true, Lynda Fisher put a lot of extra hours in at her office. She needed to rest, relax, recover from a long workweek, not spend this one day off doing heavy lawn work and home fix-it projects. It was on the tip of his tongue to suggest that she hire someone to do the work, but just as quickly he changed his mind.

The Fisher sisters' house was well kept, decorated tastefully, but it was modest in both size and furnishings. He'd pried a little more information about Lynda and her sister out of Theresa earlier that day. Their parents had left them very little. To make matters worse, Suzanne's husband had deserted her shortly before the second little girl was born, and Lynda had stepped in, providing a home and, more recently, tuition for Suzanne's schooling.

It appeared Lynda was not only head of the family but also the main breadwinner. Lynda was probably doing well for a relatively new practitioner. However, given the unusual circumstances and responsibilities, it stood to reason she could ill afford the hired help for various household tasks that he and Theresa had taken for granted in their growing-up years.

Kent put his plans immediately into action. The romantic dinner for two he planned to end the day with was still a very real possibility. "If I help you, we'll get done in half the time. Allowing for some cleanup time of ourselves, maybe a recuperative nap, we ought to be able to have dinner around . . . say, seven?"

"Can't you take no for an answer?"

"No."

How hard could mowing the lawn be? Kent had asked himself when he'd volunteered for yard duty. He'd never done it, but he understood the principle. He'd asked himself the same thing about trimming a hedge and given himself the same answer. It wasn't as if he'd never done any domestic chores. He'd had a period of totally "doing for himself." During those years he'd hacked around the country with a jazz band

that never quite made it, he'd made just enough
money to keep body and soul together.

Out of necessity and stubbornness to make it on his
own, he'd learned to cook, clean and do his own
laundry. Later he'd found the experience helpful when
he'd put himself through college. If he could run a
vacuum sweeper, surely he could run a lawn mower.
Hedge trimmers were nothing more than a huge pair
of scissors. Lynda's yard wasn't very big, and the
hedge wasn't very long. The job could be done in an
hour, two at the most.

The sun was shining red and low through the trees
when Kent carried the last bag of clippings to the curb.
He was covered with sweat, and every inch of his skin
felt as if there were grass stuck to it. A sharp, hot pain
knifed between his shoulder blades. Muscles in his
legs, arms and back burned. And he'd thought an
hour of raquetball was a workout!

After five—he checked his watch—six hours of yard
work, nothing appealed to him except a long shower
followed by hours of soaking in a Jacuzzi. And the
sight of Lynda's beautifully rounded derriere point-
ing toward the sky. She was bent over, collecting grass
clippings. Her T-shirt was perspiration soaked and
stuck to her like a second skin, revealing the shallow
dent down her lower back and the shape of her
breasts.

He was busy concentrating on putting one foot in
front of the other when Lynda straightened. She lifted
her arms overhead and stretched. He felt a twinge of
male appreciation for the lines of her lithe body. When
she dropped her arms, shook them and rolled her
head, he felt more than a twinge.

The sight of the wisp of golden hair that curled innocently at her nape was like an aphrodisiac. He was so aware of her as a woman, the most desirable he'd ever encountered. The thought of brushing aside that little curl and kissing that delicate spot on her neck had him stifling a moan in anticipation. Arousal hit him, fast and hard. He was glad for the latest ache in his body. He was still alive, and some parts of his body were functioning normally.

"How about a long soak in a Jacuzzi?" he suggested, imagining it as the perfect after-dinner activity for more reasons than easing the stiffness of their over-taxed muscles.

Her eyes closed, Lynda continued rolling her head and flexing her shoulders. "Hmm...sounds like heaven," she murmured, and Kent couldn't agree more. His plans for a candlelight dinner for two were looking more promising.

"Thanks for all your help today. I couldn't have done all the house repairs if I'd had to do the hedge myself."

"You're welcome. Now, about dinner," he began, his fatigue lifting with each passing moment he stood beside her. "I should be able to get home, clean up and be back here in an hour. Will that give you enough time?"

"It should. Hot dogs all right with you?"

"Hot dogs?"

"You don't like hot dogs?" she asked, her eyes wide with incredulity, as if he'd just confessed to something close to treason.

"Sure, I do," Kent returned quickly. He was getting the uncomfortable feeling his plans for the evening were being dramatically altered. Hot dogs weren't at all what he had in mind for the menu. While he'd been working, he'd taken a mental inventory of his pantry and wine cellar. Quiche with champagne or Steak Diane with a sauvignon were the possibilities that sprang to mind.

"Good. I can't thank you enough for your help today."

"I was glad to do it. I enjoyed it." He meant every word. Aching muscles and all, he had enjoyed himself.

They'd divided up the chores and worked side by side all afternoon, with some good-natured teasing over each other's abilities at times, and sometimes just going quietly about their separate tasks. The work had been physically taxing, but it had also been satisfying. He'd decided midway through the afternoon that there was a lot to be said for the typical suburban homeowner's life-style. He'd also come to realize Lynda was more than a challenge to him; she was a woman he actually liked and felt very at home with—a totally new experience in his relatively vast experience with women.

"It won't be anything fancy, just a family barbecue in the backyard," Lynda said, heading for the back gate. She sent him a dazzling smile. "See you in an hour. Suzanne and the girls should be back by then."

The redwood gate clicked closed, and Kent was left in the middle of the driveway wondering how she'd railroaded him so easily.

Lynda stood with a smile of triumph on her face. How's it feel to have the table turned, big guy? she asked silently. She'd taken control right out of his hands, adeptly outmaneuvered him and had him doing something completely opposite to his plans.

Feeling more like her usual self than she had since her fateful birthday, Lynda's step was light as she entered her house and headed for a shower. She was back in control. Her life was going as she'd planned and wanted. Kent Berringer was just a man. He had no magical powers over her. They'd spent hours together, and not once had she dissolved into a mindless puddle of desire.

She was just stepping out of the shower when she heard the voices of her nieces and sister. She dried quickly, stepped into her terry robe and headed down the hall. "Hey, guys, how was the zoo?" she asked as she entered the kitchen and confronted two exuberant little girls and two dusty, tired adults.

"We saw everything there was to see," Theresa announced, sinking her clearly exhausted body into a kitchen chair. The sophisticated woman who'd appeared on her doorstep earlier that day dressed in a crisp, immaculate designer outfit was gone. Bright orange streaks of what had probably been a dripping popsicle plus some dusty smudges marred her now-rumpled clothes. The blue-black hair that had hung like midnight silk down her back was fastened with a rubber band at her nape. She looked as much like a suburban mommy as Kent had looked like a suburban homeowner when he'd left.

The Berringer siblings had put in quite a day, Lynda decided. She judged that trudging through one of the country's major zoos with two small children had been as foreign to Theresa as trimming a hedge had been to Kent. And yet, they'd both come through their trials with good grace and seemed to have truly enjoyed themselves. Lynda was struck again with the thought that there was far more to Kent than he'd revealed.

Remembering his comments that the Berringers were a very proper family, Lynda took some quick assessments of Theresa and her brother. *Class* was the first word that came to mind. It was written all over both of them. The way they talked, dressed, conducted themselves. There was an air of refinement about them that smacked of old money, and Lynda added another entry onto her list of reasons why Kent Berringer was a man to be avoided.

Papa had come from that kind of background, too. Growing up never having to worry about money had resulted in his never worrying about it as an adult, even after his poor investments had obliterated the wealth he'd inherited. He'd been handsome, cultured, charismatic, extravagant and lots of fun. He'd also been as irresponsible as he'd been irresistible.

Kent Berringer had all the earmarks of being a reincarnation of Gerald Fisher, and Lynda knew her survival depended on her ability to guard her heart against the man. Unlike her mother, Lynda wasn't going into a relationship blind. She knew what lay at the end of the primrose path.

"We didn't see no pandas! They're still in China!"

Moe's petulant statement broke into Lynda's thoughts, and she was reminded of why she'd dashed down to greet the zoo returnees in the first place. "Would hot dogs on the grill help hold you over until the pandas get here in a couple of years?" she asked.

Moe's face lit up. "And ice-cream bars?" she asked, as if she needed further persuasion.

Lynda looked to Suzanne and received an agreeable nod. "Yep," she told her niece. "Theresa? Would you like to stay for dinner? Kent will be here, too," she announced to the gratification of the two matchmakers. Let them gloat, Lynda thought smugly. It'll be short-lived. This evening's family picnic would surely be the last time she and Kent would be in each other's company.

Seven

"You look fantastic this morning," Suzanne said in compliment as Lynda entered the kitchen on Thursday morning.

"You're beautiful, Aunt Lyndy," Arrie added with something akin to awe.

"And you smell pretty, too," was Moe's addition when Lynda took her place beside her at the breakfast table.

"You all sound as if my appearance today is a surprise," Lynda said, reaching for a glass of orange juice. "Have I been looking bad lately?"

"Quite the contrary, sis," Suzanne remarked as she joined the family at the table. "You always look good. It's just that this week, you've been looking terrific...more so by the day."

Lynda saw her sister, dimples flashing merrily, give her a thorough perusal. She was aware of the soft wispy curls that framed her face, softening the severity of how her hair was secured at the nape of her neck with a clip. A peach shirtwaist of soft, silky fabric draped her body; the color made her skin glow and the cut of the dress hinted subtly at the curves. A paisley scarf fastened at her shoulder with a gold pin that matched her earrings provided accent and the finishing touch. The overall effect was as stunning as it was stylish, far more stylish than the usual skirts and blouses she wore to the office, except this week. Starting with Monday, each day had seen the steady emergence of accessories long neglected and of a bit more attention to hair and makeup.

"I like," Suzanne stated, giving an all-encompassing wave of her hand. "New?"

Lynda squirmed uncomfortably, having second thoughts about the ensemble. Maybe it was too much for the office. She glanced up at the clock above the sink. It was too late to change, she she really didn't want to. She felt good in this dress.

"I had a little extra time at lunch yesterday. There was a sale, and I thought my wardrobe could use an uplift. You know, dress for success," she offered as rationalization for the shopping spree.

"To match your more successful social life, by chance?"

"That has—" Lynda halted the denial that had sprung defensively. It would have been a lie, and Suzanne would have been quick to call her on it. Any claim that Kent's consistent arrival at Lynda's office each evening at six had absolutely nothing to do with the subtle changes she'd been making in her appearance would have been an exercise in futility in the face of her sister's obvious insight.

The truth was, the little changes and extra efforts she'd been taking with her clothing, hair and makeup had been unconscious until the family had called attention to them this morning. After all, Kent wasn't her kind of man. She didn't even like him, so why would she want to impress him? If anything, she wanted to discourage him.

Who was she kidding? she asked herself. Not Suzanne, that was for sure. Her matchmaking sister was wearing expressions of growing triumph each day.

"You don't have to call and tell me you're not going to be home for supper again tonight. I already know you won't be here," Suzanne said.

"That's assuming I'm going out again tonight, which I have no plans of doing," Lynda said, wondering why the statement produced a small stab of disappointment.

"Sure, sure, sure," Suzanne teased. "The man shows up Monday, Tuesday and Wednesday, and you think he's not going to on Thursday? For a bright woman, you're awfully dense."

"Even if he does, I'm not going. Dr. Kelsey is back in the office this week part-time. Most of the responsibility of the practice is still on my shoulders. I'm already behind in the paperwork, and getting more behind each day. I can't afford any more time with that man."

There were other demands on her time besides her career. Her family needed her, too. Much like a conscientious husband leaving his wife alone night after night, she felt guilty leaving Suzanne to cope with two rambunctious youngsters all alone each evening. Her sister put in long hours each day, too; her classes in the morning followed by five hours of working at the veterinary clinic in the afternoon.

"You need some adult companionship in the evening," she told her sister. "I'll come straight home tonight, I promise. I can go back to the office for a couple of hours after the girls go to bed."

"Not necessary, but thanks for being so sweet about helping with the kids," Suzanne said as she gathered up the children's things and her own books. "I'm not going to be exactly alone with the little critters anyway. Jay's taking us out for pizza tonight, so even if you did come home, you'd have to eat all by yourself or come with us."

Lynda had been almost through the back door but that divulgence had stopped her. "Jay? He was here Tuesday night, too, wasn't he? Seems to me you're seeing quite a lot of Mr. Holland," she said, and had the satisfaction of seeing her sister squirm for a change. "Something going on here that I don't know about?"

"Maybe," was Suzanne's reply, accompanied by a starry-eyed look. It was the look, more than the implication of the one-word reply, that aroused immediate concern in Lynda. She couldn't bear to see her sister go through anything like her marriage again. "Be careful," she warned, wanting to say so much more, and would have if there had been time.

"I'm a lot older and wiser, and Jay isn't anything like Rick," Suzanne said, but Lynda felt far from assured. "Get going or you're going to be late. And have a good time tonight."

"Why do I keep letting him talk me into this?" Lynda grumbled as she lowered herself into the low-slung red sports car parked at the curb in front of her office. Once again, she'd let Kent whisk her away from her office when she should have stayed there. With Suzanne and the girls engaged for dinner, she could've sent out for a sandwich and attended to that pile of paperwork she'd told her sister about.

The pace that had been set since Monday had to stop soon or there would be no hope that she'd ever catch up. The way things were looking, she was going to have to work at her desk most of the weekend. Dr. Kelsey was going to see the Saturday-morning patients, and this weekend would have been her first entirely free one for over two months.

Monday had marked the return of some normalcy, or so Lynda had hoped. Dr. Kelsey's return even for just a half day had freed Lynda to concentrate on what was not only her specialty but to her the most gratifying area of optometry—children's vision. Though it meant more work, it was work she enjoyed, for she knew the time spent preparing the lengthy reports benefited her young patients and enhanced her reputation in the professional world.

Consequently, all was close to right in her little world, she'd thought—until Kent had shown up at the end of office hours. She'd been sure that Sunday had ended a brief and totally frivolous relationship with Kenton J. Berringer. After all, she'd spent all of that day giving him a sample of what her life was like. First, she'd worked him half to death in the yard, then subjected him to the circus that was the family backyard barbecue at the Fisher household. The only goodnight kisses he'd received had been from Arrie and Moe.

When Kent had made an attempt to linger after the meal, she'd announced that she was spending the evening at her office. After thanking him once again for his help with the yard work, she'd grabbed her car keys and left. Once at her office, she'd immersed herself so thoroughly in her work that she'd done a pretty good job of convincing herself that the interlude was over.

She didn't have the time to pursue a relationship with a man right now. Even if she'd had the time, Kent was as wrong for her as she was for him. She wasn't a really fun person, not his kind at all. Sunday should have proved to him that what they'd shared Saturday had been a fluke.

It hadn't. If anything, he'd stepped up his pursuit of her. The man was utterly obtuse. Every day, he'd shown up, she'd said no, he'd insisted, and within minutes she'd been driven to the restaurant where he worked, Trafalgar Square, where he'd set a pattern. First, dinner together, then Kent would join the rest of Berringer Brass and begin the club's evening entertainment. At a break between sets, Kent would walk her to a waiting taxi, kiss her senseless and tuck her into the vehicle that promptly took her back to the office. No more. No less.

She continued to insist that she didn't want to spend any time with him and that he wasn't the kind of man she wanted in her life. Except for the short moments in his arms at the end of each evening, she never changed her stance, and he never ceased to ignore it.

As soon as Kent had settled himself behind the wheel, Lynda asked, "Why do you keep showing up like this?"

"Why?" The smile that had been on his face vanished. He looked directly into her eyes, as if he were delving beyond the surface and reaching into her soul. Lynda had the uncomfortable feeling that he saw something she didn't even know herself. "I'm not entirely sure anymore," he admitted after a moment. "Except that I can't just drop whatever's been started between us."

"Nothing's been started between us," Lynda stated stubbornly. "Why can't you accept that?"

"Because it's not the truth," he returned as he started the car. "Despite what you might think of my character, I'm really quite an honest guy. Take my word on it, something's definitely been started between us." Stopped at the traffic signal, he turned his full attention to her. "I also like to finish whatever I start."

"What if I say it's finished?" Lynda asked, growing more and more uncomfortable under the intensity of his gaze. "Today. This very minute."

"I wouldn't let you."

"Wouldn't let me?" The demand exploded from Lynda's lips. "Wouldn't let me?" she repeated as she searched for words to express her anger at his high-handedness. "Don't you ever consider anyone's feelings but your own?"

"Quite often and especially in this case," he returned smoothly, his attention once again on the traffic now that the signal had changed. "I don't think you really want to stay away from me, because if you did, nothing I could have said or done, short of throwing you over my shoulder, would consistently get you out of your office and on the way to dinner at the club with me. Strange as it might seem to you, I happen to think you're a very strong-minded woman who can't be pushed into anything you don't really want to do.''

"I don't really want to go out to dinner with you. I haven't all week," Lynda asserted, but the words didn't come out as strongly as she would have liked, nor did they ring true to her ears.

Kent's response was a skeptically raised eyebrow, and Lynda shifted uncomfortably in her seat. He grinned at her, and she struggled to keep from grinning right back. Allowing only a hint of a smile, she admitted, "Okay, a gourmet dinner at Trafalgar Square is infinitely better than a carry-out sandwich at my desk or tuna casserole at home." A streak of stubborn independence prompted her to add, "But I absolutely have to get back to the office right after dinner. I intend to put in an hour or two before I go home."

Kent controlled the chuckle that threatened to erupt. She insisted every night that she had to get back to her office right after dinner. And every night it took very little persuasion on his part to convince her to stay a little longer. "Will you stay for the first set?" he asked, as he always did.

His tone, full of hope and an eagerness to please, was her continual undoing. After four steady nights of it, she was disgusted with herself that she hadn't developed any resistance. "I'll stay for the first set, but only if I have your solemn word that you'll make it a short one and won't even attempt to persuade me to stay longer," she bargained.

"Would you stay longer if I were to attempt some form of persuasion?"

"Did anyone ever tell you that you have an extraordinarily large ego?"

"You. Could I persuade you to stay longer?"

"Egotist!"

Kent's chuckle was exactly the same as what she'd had to endure the afternoon they'd met—deep, rich, male and knowing. It caused the same conflicting reactions in her now as it had then. A part of her warned her to stay away. At the same time, another part of her was warmed all over by it and wanted to throw herself into his arms, the consequences of such a foolhardy and dangerous action be damned.

It was a classic love/hate relationship, she judged as she lapsed into silence. When she realized where her thoughts had led, she gasped and sat bolt upright. Love/hate? Her feelings toward Kent were neither! They weren't that powerful!

"Something wrong?" Kent inquired, noticing her sudden agitation.

Yes! You! Us! Her mind was in turmoil, and she grabbed at the most logical explanation for her gasp and rigid position. "You're going pretty fast, aren't you?"

"I'm driving exactly the speed limit—thirty-five."

"Sorry. Guess it seems faster in a car this low to the ground," she muttered, her thoughts racing. She didn't hate Kent. He'd done nothing to warrant such a strong negative emotion. Love? Hardly. She didn't even like him ... well, maybe she did. It would be impossible not to like someone as charming as Kent Berringer.

But, her conscience reminded her, a woman didn't respond to a man's kisses the way she responded to Kent's if she felt only like for the man. Working through her reactions and feelings toward Kent Berringer with logic, Lynda kept coming up with love as the answer.

No! every fiber of her being screamed. Chemistry, a purely physical reaction between two healthy attractive people, was the only logical answer. Love didn't happen in less than a week, and love was impossible between two people as diametrically different in outlook on life as she and Kent.

She'd been unaware that she'd been wringing her hands until Kent reached over and covered them with his. "Something is the matter," he stated. "What is it?"

"Uh...tell me about Jay Holland," she blurted. "He's been seeing a lot of Suzanne lately."

"And you want to know if he's suitable company for your sister, right?"

Lynda shrugged sheepishly, relieved that they were talking about something that could take her mind off her own inner anguish. "Well, yes. I don't want to see Suzanne hurt."

"She's a big girl. She can take care of herself," he stated, essentially echoing what Suzanne had implied just that morning. Lynda was no more assured now than she'd been hours before. Consequently, she responded with a statement to that effect.

"Settle down," Kent ordered, gently patting her hands before returning his to the steering wheel. "You sound more like a parent than a sister."

"Habit," Lynda admitted begrudgingly. "Mother's basically the role I've played in her life since she was six."

"Even parents have to let go sometime," Kent said, again essentially echoing another of Suzanne's recent statements. "But if it'll make you feel any better, I'll tell you about Jay.

"I've known him since the first day of kindergarten, and we went all through school together. We were in the same Cub Scout den, Boy Scout troop, Little League baseball teams and high school football team. He's a graduate of Miami University of Ohio, is a damned fine stock broker, and though I don't know his bank balance, I'd imagine it's pretty healthy. He's never been married, doesn't have a police record, and I've never seen a dog or a little kid who wasn't crazy about him. Feel better?"

"I guess I should," she said slowly, thinking over the details of the character profile Kent had just given her. Though it had been about Jay, it had also revealed almost as much about Kent. "Dogs and children aren't always good judges of character, but since you chose to use them as such, how do they feel about you?"

Kent laughed. "Neither has ever bitten me."

She had only his word about his relationship with dogs, but she knew about children. Arrie and Moe had climbed all over Kent Sunday evening. They'd plopped themselves on either side of him during the meal and regaled him with details of nearly every animal they'd seen at the zoo that day.

He'd been endearingly patient with them, even the barrage of hugs and good-night kisses they'd delivered before Suzanne had dragged them into the house and tucked them into bed. The sight of him with a little girl tucked on each side of him as he'd read them a story after dinner had been endearing. It had been difficult for Lynda to keep any emotional barricade against him later, when he'd so obviously wanted to be alone with her.

Dogs and little children had loved her father, too, Lynda remembered and quickly dismissed the two groups as character references. Papa had been wonderful with children, fun, affectionate. When she'd been small, she'd adored him. However, he'd not been the greatest of parents. As charming and lovable as he'd been, the man had not been dependable or able to provide anything remotely close to stability for his family. And Lynda knew that those two things were most needed by a child.

A woman needed them, too. Though she'd tried, Lynda's mother hadn't been successful in hiding her frequent bouts of worry and disappointment from her eldest daughter. The aneurysm that had taken her mother's life so suddenly and without warning had spared her of Gerald Fisher's growing steadily less responsible toward his family and less successful in his business dealings.

Even as young as she'd been during the eight-year interim between her parents' deaths, Lynda had been aware that her father's decline was less a result of her mother's death as it was an increasing awareness of his own ineptitude and general disenchantment with life. Almost immediately, she'd questioned if his fatal car crash had actually been an accident.

"You're awfully quiet," Kent remarked as he ushered her through the heavy carved doors of Trafalgar Square. "Stop worrying about your sister and Jay. Trust me. He's a good guy. You have my word on it."

"Now why doesn't that reassure me?" she gibed, forcing herself to abandon the dark memories of her parents. The past was best left there, her parents' mistakes left buried with it. If she was in the company of a man who seemed a reincarnation of Gerald Fisher, she'd enjoy the moment and all that was delightful about him, but carefully protect her heart from the disaster and inevitable disappointments of any lengthy attachment.

"I don't know. I keep telling you I'm an honest, law-abiding, trustworthy man."

"And you were a Boy Scout, too," she added as she slipped into their usual intimate booth near the stage.

"Yep," he agreed as he slid in beside her. "Physically strong, mentally aware and morally straight."

She raised a jaundiced eyebrow and asked sardonically, "What did you earn your merit badges in?"

He sent her a leer. "Come over to my place later and I'll show you my sash."

"The Boy Scouts of America will strip them from you when they find out you use them for such a lure," she teased.

Dramatically, he placed his hand over his heart. "I'm wounded, and you should be ashamed. How could you suggest there was anything prurient in my invitation! I had absolutely nothing else in mind but showing off my Eagle Scout badge."

"Sure you did," she drawled, totally immersed in and enjoying their repartee. In fact, once she'd finished her obligatory grumbling about his high-handed methods of getting her out of her office and the equally obligatory claims that she couldn't afford the time away from her desk, she thoroughly enjoyed their evenings together.

Kent was witty, a smooth conversationalist, knowledgeable about a variety of subjects from current events to trivia, even old movies, a category in which she was an expert. He was the perfect gentleman, debonair and so good looking she couldn't help but feel she was the envy of many of the women in the club each night. His company wasn't all she enjoyed each evening. The music, especially his playing, was divine. She loved jazz, especially the old standards.

Though the first night when he'd dedicated the last number of the set, "Dreamsville," to her, she'd been uncomfortable with the attention the audience had given her, she'd become less uncomfortable each evening because she knew what was to come. A few measures into the piece she, like everyone else in the club, gave herself up to the smooth tones so appropriately titled, and she was sorry when it ended, sorrier still that it was the final selection she could stay for and that her listening pleasure was over.

Every evening, it took every ounce of willpower she owned to resist staying longer. Was it any wonder, then, that with the notes of Mancini's dreamy melody still echoing through her mind, she literally floated out of the restaurant on Kent's arm and succumbed so easily to the sensual magic of his embraces? Willpower was evidently handed out in finite amounts, and Lynda had come to the frightening realization as the week progressed that her allotted portion wasn't generous.

Eight

Lynda hung up her lab jacket and glanced at her watch. Fifteen minutes until six. Butterflies swarmed in her stomach, and every inch of her flesh felt tingly. Unsnapping the hair clip at her nape, she ducked into the lavoratory. She had fifteen minutes to freshen up. Fifteen minutes until—

Until what? Kent Berringer arrived to take her to dinner? She had no guarantee of that. Last night when he'd helped her into the taxi, he'd said nothing about seeing her again. He'd said nothing the other nights, but he'd consistently arrived at six o'clock all week, she reminded herself. So why should tonight be any different?

"Because tonight you're openly admitting you're looking forward to spending the evening with him and you're suddenly afraid you're going to be disappointed," she said aloud as she stared at her reflec-

tion in the mirror. She'd already flicked a brush
through her hair. It hung loose around her shoulders,
framing her face with waves, and it was going to stay
that way for the rest of the evening—because she knew
Kent liked it that way.

A blusher brush was in her hand, poised to add
color she didn't really need tonight. Her cheeks were
already flushed with excitement.

"What's happening to you?" she asked the woman
in the mirror, afraid she already knew the answer.

Hanging in a clothing bag in the lavoratory was the
dress she was about to change into, bought at noon
today, especially for tonight. The teal-blue silk had
been on sale, but she would have paid top dollar for it
if it hadn't been. The simple, sleeveless style was exactly what she'd been looking for. The color was perfect for her. Kent will love it, had been her thought
when she'd walked out of the store.

"Oh, Lord." She gasped and grabbed the sink for
support. She was dressing to please that man. Styling
her hair to please that man. Thinking about him
throughout the day, dreaming about him at night. Her
"date" with him tonight had been the single most important thing on her mind and her driving force all
day.

"You fool!" she chided the woman in the mirror,
and helpless to stop her, watched her reach for the top
button on her blouse. The fool knew she'd better hurry
if she was going to be ready on time. A tiny sane being
imprisoned deep within the fool's body shuddered at
how this fool was coming so dangerously close to depending on Kent Berringer to complete her day properly.

"He certainly does know how to complete a woman's day properly," the fool said flippantly, a silly, dreamy smile on her face that nearly sent the sane being into apoplexy.

Totally ignoring the critical condition of her sanity, Lynda went about freshening up and applying a liberal amount of the new perfume she'd purchased the day she'd bought the peach dress. Slipping into the new teal dress and accessories, she relived every second of the final moments she'd spent with Kent the night before.

After wooing her senses with mellow tones during the first set, he'd returned immediately to their booth and pulled her gently and wordlessly to her feet. Instead of escorting her directly outside to the waiting taxi as he usually did each evening, he'd guided her into a small office. He'd turned on only the desk lamp then locked the door. "No parking-lot good-night kisses tonight," he had said as he'd wrapped his arm around her waist and drawn her close. "That's no way to say a proper good-night."

Held captive by the fire burning in the cobalt depths of his eyes, she'd returned his scrutiny for a long moment before nodding her head. As if he'd been waiting for her assent, he'd instantly lowered his head toward hers.

At the first touch of his lips on hers, Lynda had opened, welcoming the immediate possession he'd always taken of her mouth, but he'd surprised her by brushing her lips with his, then flicking his tongue along their outline instead. "I want to savor you," he'd said between soft caresses of his mouth across hers, her cheeks, her throat. While his mouth had tantalized, his hands had aroused her as they moved in small circles over her back and hips.

"Ever since you gave up your grumbling and started smiling tonight, I've wanted to do this," he'd said, and kissed the corners of her mouth. "And this." He'd pressed his lips to the faint dimple in her left cheek and to the other just below the corner of her right eye.

"With each taste of your food, each sip of your wine, I wanted to taste you," he'd murmured against her lips, then took the possession she'd been yearning for. His tongue had invited a mating with hers, and she'd given it willingly, eagerly. Slipping her hands beneath his jacket, she'd slid her palms to his chest, pausing to measure the beat of his heart, and then let her fingertips slide between the buttons of his shirt to feel his warmth and texture without barriers.

He'd groaned in response to the first touch of her fingers on his flesh. At the sound of his pleasure, she'd felt the protective barriers she'd thrown up against the man disappear, and a sensual need mixed with feminine possessiveness take their place. Emboldened, she'd slipped two of his shirt buttons open and slid her hand farther inside.

He'd groaned again and lifted his mouth from hers. Inviting her with his eyes, he'd pulled her with him toward the sofa lined against the wall. Though she'd followed, she'd said weakly, "My taxi."

"Not for another ten minutes," he'd informed her, his voice not quite steady as he'd urged her downward. His fingers hadn't been very steady, either, when he opened the buttons of her shirtwaist. Hovering above her for a moment, he'd brushed aside the fronts of her dress, then lowered his head to kiss the slope of her breasts. One flick of his fingers and the front fastening of her bra had come open, freeing her entirely for the touch of Kent's fingers and mouth.

The slide of the new teal silk dress over Lynda's skin now recalled the memory of Kent's silken caresses on her flesh. Her breasts felt warm and heavy. Her nipples tingled.

Swallowing hard, Lynda tried to dispel the memory of those minutes on the sofa. Nothing in her previous experience had prepared her for last night. They hadn't made love, but she'd come so close to the ecstasy of fulfillment. She didn't need to look in the mirror to know that her cheeks were flushed and her eyes overly bright.

Kent might not be the right man for her for the long term, but he was the right man to release the part of her that had been relegated to a closed closet during most of her adult years. She was content with all he offered, for she knew he was for only now. She couldn't afford anything more than a temporary affair with him.

"And it will be only temporary," she firmly warned the flush-cheeked fool who looked back at her in the mirror.

Kent's eyes widened, and he let out a long, low whistle when Lynda walked into the waiting room. "You look...are beautiful," he said as he advanced on her. "If you start that bit about having to stay here and work on whatever it is you claim is piling up on your desk, I'm going to stand here and watch your nose grow a foot."

"My nose is going to stay exactly its usual length," she said, returning his smile. The worries and doubts that had assailed her earlier were evaporating in the light of his appreciative smile. They were replaced by an inner glow, a warm feeling that she was desired. Kent's smile held more than appreciation. A sensuous flame burned in his eyes, heating every part of Lynda that designated her a woman.

"Good. I like your nose exactly the way it is." To punctuate his statement, he kissed the tip of her nose. Then he kissed her hands and placed them on his shoulders. "I like almost everything about you," he said, slipping his arms around her waist and drawing her into an embrace.

"Almost?" she asked, arching her upper body away from him to avoid the kiss she knew was coming.

Sliding one hand to the middle of her back, Kent overcame her resistance easily. "Everything but your insistence all week that you'd rather work than go out with me," he said against her lips.

"I haven't mentioned work this evening," she reminded softly, and felt his answer, a smile and the murmur of her name.

His mouth covered hers hungrily. As always the feel of his lips on hers sent waves of desire through her entire body. Her knees weakened, and she wrapped her arms around his shoulders for support. She responded eagerly to the demands of his mouth, opening to the invasion of his tongue and then returning the sensuous assault.

Knowing he was fast approaching the moment of no return and that this was not the time or the place, Kent eased his mouth reluctantly from hers. He could feel a trembling and wasn't sure whether it was Lynda's or his own. Slowly, he relaxed his hold on her, pressed his lips to her forehead and asked, "You will come with me tonight?"

Though unsure of all she might be agreeing to, Lynda nodded her head. "I need to get my purse," she said huskily, stepping away from him on shaky legs. "It's back in my private office." She turned slowly and walked off.

Kent's senses were whirling as he waited for her. From the moment she'd walked into the waiting room to greet him, he'd sensed a difference in her. It wasn't just her appearance, though the dress should have been his first clue. The silky little number wasn't designed for office wear. It revealed far too much cleavage. It appeared to wrap one and a half times around her and was secured with only one fastening at her waist. He'd have to be blind not to guess she'd dressed for their evening together.

The real difference had been her open expression of genuine happiness at seeing him. Kent hadn't realized how much he'd wanted it. From the beginning, she'd been a challenge to him. There had been the challenge to break past her barriers and find the sensuous woman beneath. He found that sensuous woman every time he held her in his arms. She was the answer to a man's dreams.

That had led to the second challenge: proving that "a man like him" was what she needed. It was looking very much as if she was pretty well convinced. He'd wanted her to reach out to him, admit that there was something very special and powerful between them. Tonight, she wasn't denying it.

So why didn't he feel really good about that particular victory? he wondered as he began to pace the waiting room. He'd discovered a woman he wanted very much, was beginning to think he might love, and she was returning those feelings. She didn't know who his family was and knew nothing about his law practice. She was falling for the real Kent Berringer, the man beneath the trappings of wealth, social status and success. For some inexplicable reason, he had the distinct feeling he wasn't entirely satisfied.

"I'm ready," Lynda announced as she reappeared in the waiting room, her purse in hand.

He certainly hoped so, Kent thought, setting aside his doubts. Grinning, he held out his arm. "Come away with me, my lovely," he invited, and was delighted when, without a moment's hesitation, she glided to his side and slipped her arm through his.

Fearful that she might still put up even a slight show of resistance, he got her out of her office immediately. They were out of the building, into his car and pulling away from the curb in record time.

"In a hurry?" Lynda looked questioningly at Kent.

"Just don't believe in wasting time."

"*You* don't believe in wasting time?" She laughed scoffingly.

He shrugged sheepishly. "I believe in efficiency."

She sent him a disbelieving look, but decided to let the subject drop. "I'm curious about Trafalgar Square. I've noticed that the club is filled close to capacity even on weeknights. That's pretty remarkable for any restaurant, but especially for such a new one."

"It's beginning to look like one of the best investments I ever—"

"You own it?"

Lynda's question prevented him from divulging that the supper club had been one of his suggested investments to the Capital City Bank board of directors: his family. "I'm just one of many investors," he explained, feeling a small twinge of guilt. Some of his money drew interest at Capital City Bank, so he was technically an investor in the club.

"Smart investment," she complimented. "It provides you with some income and a place to play."

"Trafalgar Square's under no obligation to hire my group to play. I made sure of that," he remarked defensively. He'd drafted a short document that expressed exactly that. He wanted Berringer Brass to stand on its own merit, as much for his own satisfaction as that of its members. If he hadn't, his mother would have insisted that detail be put in the loan agreement. Her motive, even after all these years and his success in a "more acceptable" field, would have been to throw another roadblock against his performing.

Berringers were allowed to play musical instruments but not professionally, especially playing something so common as jazz. That he'd been doing it for the past several years, proving it was more than a hobby, didn't make it any more acceptable. Berringers weren't supposed to be entertainers.

Kent cursed inwardly. Here he was thirty-six years old and still bothered by his mother's disapproval. After all that time, it still made his blood boil when he thought of all the arguments they'd had. After his high-school graduation, he turned down college and hit the road to seek his fame and fortune as a jazz musician. Would he ever forget the smug look on Patricia's face when he'd come home, with a tidy bank account but still an unknown, after two years? His desire to pursue a degree in law hadn't pleased her, either; it didn't uphold the family's banking tradition. Hence, he'd put himself through school, stubbornly refusing to touch the trust fund set up for that purpose. That trust fund was still resting in the bank.

"They hired Berringer Brass because we pack in an audience. I'm good, damned good," he declared vehemently, remembering all too clearly how often he'd had to defend his ability in a field that had once been his career choice.

"Yes, you are, maybe the best I've heard," Lynda agreed, surprised at the anger she detected in Kent's voice.

Lynda's easy agreement brought Kent instantly back to reality. Calming, he apologized. "Sorry, I guess I still get pretty defensive about my playing."

"You shouldn't," she assured. "As I said before, you're good, and I know I'm not the only one who thinks so."

He took his gaze away from the traffic momentarily and grinned mischievously at her. "Yeah, I'm irresistible. The women love me."

She snorted in derision. "Not nearly as much as you love yourself," Lynda quipped.

Lynda's gibe didn't daunt Kent. "Loving oneself is a prerequisite to loving another."

Lynda countered with, " 'He that falls in love with himself will have no rivals'—Ben Franklin."

"I hadn't thought of that," Kent commented thoughtfully, as much to himself as to her. He tensed, his mind quickly rerunning her every remark and action during their brief association. Other than her continued assertions that he wasn't her type, there was nothing to indicate that there was any other reason for her continued resistance to him, especially nothing like another man in her life. He'd taken up all her free time, so it was more than doubtful there was anyone else. And she'd been ready and willing this evening. Yet, he knew from past experience both in his private and professional lives that it was never wise to assume. "Have I any rivals?"

Studying the cityscape beyond the car window, she returned with a feigned indifference, "I don't know. Anybody been throwing themselves at you lately?"

Kent relaxed, not realizing until that moment just how anxious he was about her answer. He'd been ninety-nine percent sure there was no other man in her life, but early in his career as an attorney, he'd been tripped up by the one percent detail left to chance. "You're the only one throwing herself at me," he stated baldly, purely to gain her full attention. He got it.

"I have not!" she denied hotly.

"Sure you have." The smile that accompanied his audacious assertion was the thousand watter, and Lynda felt her pulse rate increase.

He went on to explain, "Women have known since Eve that the most successful way to gain a man's attention is to offer an irresistible challenge. You, Dr. Fisher—" he reached over and tweaked one of the soft curls snuggled against her throat "—are the biggest challenge I've ever met. It's obvious, you're after me, and have been since the first minute."

Lynda began to laugh.

"You laugh at the truth?" Kent looked as if he'd just been handed the greatest of insults, except his eyes gave him away. Despite the low, seductive lighting in the car, Lynda could see the mischievous twinkle that glittered in the middle of their cobalt depths before he turned his attention back to the highway.

"I'm laughing at your vanity," she informed him. "It's the only cure for such an extreme case."

"Ah, but that's not all Bergson said," Kent began, greatly surprising her by identifying the philosopher she'd paraphrased. "He also said, 'the only fault that's laughable is vanity.' Therefore, since I'm not a vain man nor have I told a joke, I'd appreciate a cessation of this mirth."

His request was delivered with such exaggerated formality that Lynda's laughter only intensified.

"That's it, woman." Abruptly, he steered onto the shoulder, brought the car to an immediate stop and pulled the emergency brake. "You leave me no choice," he warned.

Swiftly he leaned over and captured her face between his palms. Just as swiftly he smothered her laughter beneath the pressure of his lips. A few more giggles gurgled up her throat, then her senses reeled and her consciousness ebbed until nothing existed in her thoughts but the pleasure and excitement of his mouth. The gentle massage of his fingertips on her temples sent currents of delight throughout her body. When he finally lifted his mouth from hers, she was incapable of laughter, speech or thought.

Brushing her throbbing lips with his thumbs, Kent held her captive with his eyes. His gaze was as soft as the caress of his thumbs. His voice was low and halting when he said, "That was some appetizer. I'm ravenous."

"Then I think we'd better get this car moving again. There's not a waiter in sight," she suggested, wanting to break his sensual hold on her but not having the strength to move her face away from the warm palms that held it so tenderly.

"Right." Kent dropped his hands and grabbed at sanity while he waited for a break in the traffic. Lynda concentrated on bringing her breathing under control.

Once on their way again, they rode in silence, neither quite capable of speech. It was Lynda who finally broke the quiet. "Did you study philosophy at college?" she asked, hoping to find out something more about Kent's background, his education, anything to solve the mystery of the man. None of the fragments she knew about him fell together to form a whole that made sense.

"It was my major," Kent admitted.

"That's an awfully impractical major unless—" Lynda frowned as she realized they weren't headed for Trafalgar Square. "Where are we going?" she demanded.

"We're going to Granville, didn't I tell you?" he inquired calmly.

"No, you didn't tell me," Lynda said. "Why Granville? What about Trafalgar Square? Aren't you playing there tonight?"

"The Granville Inn is a nice place to go, and I thought you'd enjoy it," he explained, answering her first question. Smiling, he wondered if he'd made a tactical error by not apprising her of his plans. No, that would've been a bigger error, he rationalized. She'd been ready and willing to go out with him tonight, but he was sure she would have balked at his plans. Springing it on her was the only way. For some reason, the woman seemed compelled to continually insist that she didn't want what he suspected she most definitely did—him.

You'd better hope so, or you're going to qualify as the biggest jerk in the world, his conscience warned, and Kent felt a prickle of guilt at the back of his neck.

"No problem with the club," he said, answering her second question. "That gig was over last night."

"So you're opening at The Granville Inn tonight?"

"No," he answered simply, wishing his conscience would leave him alone. "Berringer Brass doesn't have another gig scheduled for several weeks."

"Can you afford to be off that long?"

Her query was the perfect opportunity for him to tell her the complete truth about himself. Only the timing was wrong. It was too soon...or so he rationalized. He'd been burned before, not often, and not for several years. He'd learned to protect himself against women who were more impressed by his wealth and status than the man beneath the trappings.

He didn't really think Lynda was that shallow, nor was she a groupie interested in him only because he was an entertainer. She liked jazz and had become a fan, but she'd made it abundantly clear she was opposed to any meaningful involvement with a man who was nothing more than an irregularly employed musician. That kind of man was far too undependable and smacked of "playing at life" for someone as work- and career-oriented as Lynda Fisher. And yet, they were involved. No matter what she might have claimed all week, her actions tonight indicated that their involvement was coming to be as meaningful to her as he'd come to realize it was to him.

Still, he wanted the insurance of a little more time to make sure. He hoped this weekend would do it, and so he hedged about his ability to live on the income from infrequent gigs. "I'll get by. I've got some other sources of income," he said, telling himself that it was the truth, understated, but the truth.

Nine

———

Didn't I tell you you'd like this place?" Kent asked when he and Lynda paused on the cobblestone sidewalk leading to the historic old inn.

They had arrived early for their dinner reservations, and chose to take a brief walking tour of the New England-style village. Less than thirty miles east of Columbus, Granville was a sharp contrast to the bustling metropolitan state capital. Here, time had seemingly stood still a hundred years before, when lifestyles were simpler, calmer and infinitely more gracious.

Old-fashioned streetlights glowed warmly at intervals along the tree-lined street. Century-old residences, some clapboard, others brick and stone, added their own blend of charm, some stately, others more homey. Picturesque Dennison University could be seen in the distance, its appearance and character more akin to the Ivy League institutions in the East than those of its huge younger cousin in Columbus, Ohio State University.

Lynda breathed deeply of the flower-scented evening air. A smile of contentment glowed on her features as she snuggled closer to Kent. "The inn is lovely. The whole town is lovely. I just would've appreciated some warning, maybe an invitation."

"You would've said no or put up some sort of argument," Kent retorted, his tone teasing. "To get you here, I might have had to resort to caveman techniques and you would have really been furious."

"Oh, I don't know, it might have been interesting." She smiled merrily at the look of surprise on his face.

"How interesting would you like this evening to be?" he asked casually, but the light in his eyes and the grin teasing at the corners of his mouth spelled danger with a capital *D*.

"Don't try anything," she warned as they walked through the inn's doors. "I'll sue you for assault if you bop me on the head and drag me by the hair somewhere."

"A Berringer would never stoop to anything that uncivilized," Kent informed her with mock haughtiness.

"Really?" Lynda drawled with a raised eyebrow.

"Really. Even a black-sheep Berringer, like me." Leaning close, he murmured for her ears alone, "Rendering you unconscious would take all the fun out of it." Straightening, he gave his name at the reservation desk.

Lynda was still feeling the shiver of awareness on the sensitive spot near her ear and the implication of his whispered statement when they were ushered to their table. A week, even two days before, she would have instantly squelched any assumption on his part that they might go to bed together, but tonight she had no such compulsion. Her body felt warm and liquidy, and her mind was so occupied with the delightful prospects ahead that she had trouble concentrating on the menu.

"To us." Kent lifted his wineglass and waited for her to lift hers. Tapping the rim of his glass lightly to hers, he smiled. "Tonight, a new beginning," he offered, his voice thicker and deeper than usual.

A soft smile was Lynda's response. Drinking the wine was her affirmation. Tonight was different. Instead of fighting the chemistry between them, she was embracing it. Or so Kent hoped as he gazed across the candlelit table at her.

She'd never looked more beautiful. Her eyes glowed with a warmth he would readily give all he had to bask in for the rest of his life. And the warmth was directed toward him.

His body ached with a need to hold her. Reaching over the linen-draped table, he picked up her hand and brought it to his lips. "It is a new beginning, isn't it?" he asked, needing more than his interpretation of her actions as affirmation.

"Yes" was her throatily pronounced answer, and Kent began to damn his earlier claim to civilized behavior. Throwing her over his shoulder and racing up the stairs to one of the cozy rooms on the second floor was more appealing than sitting calmly across the table from her for whatever length of time it took to get through dinner. When their first course arrived quickly, he'd never been so grateful for fast service.

"Some more champagne?" he asked, reaching for the bottle as soon as their waiter had left.

Lynda looked at her glass. It was nearly empty, and she'd barely noticed the taste of the wine that had bubbled down her throat. She'd been so bemused by her racing thoughts of how this evening would end that she'd been aware of little beyond her imaginings and the enticing man across the table.

"Champagne?" she asked.

"The only drink for celebrations," Kent informed her as he topped her glass off. "We met a week ago and..." He paused and sent her one of his deep penetrating looks that never failed to turn her limbs to water. "Since I'm not playing this evening, I'm free to spend the entire night with you."

Lynda nearly dropped the spoonful of chilled fresh vegetable soup she'd just raised to her mouth. She would have gladly traded her years of professional training for years of social experience. Here she was, thirty years old and tongue-tied because the most desirable man she'd ever met had just implied they spend the night together. To make matters worse, that was exactly what she wanted, and yet she hadn't the slightest idea how to smoothly convey her desire.

Desperate to say something, she remarked, "I've enjoyed your playing all week. I'll miss it tonight." She was surprised and relieved that her voice came out natural and steady.

"There will be other times."

Relaxing slightly, Lynda chanced a teasing, "You promise?"

"I promise and I do keep my promises," Kent vowed. Lynda sensed he was promising much more. Settling back in his chair, he smiled engagingly, effectively lightening the moment. "I promised you a nice evening at a charming restaurant, didn't I?"

"Yes, you did, and your promise is being fulfilled," she said, smiling her approval of the dishes their waiter was serving them. In truth, she didn't care what was being served for she was sure she wasn't going to be able to taste any of it. Her senses were solely attuned to Kent Berringer.

As she proceeded through the meal, she found herself reaching again and again for her champagne glass. Despite her best resolve, she was doing it again. Settling her nerves by indulging in the very stuff she'd sworn off and that had been a factor in her downfall a week ago.

But had it been such a bad fall? asked that lovesick fool inside her. No, it hadn't, the fool answered herself, and every part of Lynda agreed. That night had been a beginning that had led directly to tonight, and she was glad. Kent's entrance into her life had reminded her so very clearly that she was a woman, and she reveled in that knowledge as much as she reveled in the knowledge that he was very much a man.

"Dessert?" Kent asked, praying her answer would be no.

"None for me," she said, and he breathed an inaudible sigh of relief. He was sure he'd have gone mad engaging in even another minute of light dinner conversation. Wasn't she feeling it, too? he wondered as he signaled for the check. How could she sit there so calm and collected while he was breaking out in a cold sweat?

The Granville Inn hadn't been such a good idea after all, he decided as he placed several bills on the check tray and rose. A noisy restaurant would have been safer. Then he wouldn't be falling all over himself wondering how or if he should suggest they spend the rest of the night at the inn. He wasn't inexperienced at this sort of thing, but Lynda Fisher wasn't like any woman he'd known. She was special, and his feelings for her were special, like none he'd ever experienced.

As they left the dining room, he suggested a walk around the grounds. Beneath one of the spreading trees, he caught her up in his arms and kissed her. Her response was so instant and giving, he nearly forgot his declaration that he was a civilized man. Taking her mouth more thoroughly, he pulled her tightly to his body and was almost shaking with need when she melted against him.

"I don't want this evening to end," he muttered as he trailed kisses from her cheek to her ear.

"It doesn't have to," Lynda whispered, forging a line of soft kisses along his neck.

Stifling a moan, he set her slightly away from him and asked, "You're sure?"

Lynda caught her breath when she saw the unmistakable fires of desire flaming in his eyes, but she managed to nod her head. Abruptly, Kent scooped her up in his arms. "What are you doing?" she demanded.

"I'm making the evening interesting," he said as he started striding toward the inn.

"This isn't interesting. This is embarrassing," she stated through clenched teeth, though down deep inside she was thrilled by his audacious action. "Put me down this instant."

"This is far more romantic," he told her, and kept on walking. "I'm sure they think so, too." He nodded toward the inn's entrance.

Lynda's eyes widened at the sight of several couples emerging from the inn.

Kent didn't loosen his hold on her or alter his stride. "Smile and look as if you're enjoying this," he whispered into her ear, following his own advice by dazzling her and their audience with one of his high-wattage smiles.

More loudly, he said, "You were right, darling. This is a wonderful way to celebrate our first anniversary."

His declaration earned him a sigh and a dreamy smile from the woman at the front desk. After a minimum of paperwork, the woman placed a key in his hand, and Kent thanked her with a wink. Turning his attention back to Lynda, he quickly covered her lips with his own, effectively silencing any further words of complaint or argument.

An affair was what Lynda had decided to have with him, and spending the night with him was a part of that package. And what a delightful package it was, she decided, her pleasure overriding her embarrassment. He'd been her birthday present and was proving to be the best she'd ever received.

Kent's foot was on only the first step of the stairs when Lynda gave up pretending resistance to what she'd already agreed to. The palm that had been pressing against his shoulder began to caress the hard expanse. Her lips softened beneath his, answering his invitation with one of her own that sent Kent's senses reeling.

With only one eye open, Kent somehow managed to navigate the stairs and the hallway without ever breaking the kiss. Once inside their room, he released her legs and allowed her to slide down his body, but his hand caught her hips, pulling them against his taut thighs.

"This is why I bother with you. I love the way you resist," he murmured breathlessly before taking her mouth again. With one arm around her shoulders, he held her firmly. His other hand roamed down her back, hesitated at her waist, then smoothed over her hips.

Reveling in the tender imprisonment of his embrace, she pushed her fingers into the thick hair at his nape and cradled the back of his head. "Our first anniversary?" she teased with a skeptical lift of her eyebrow when she was able to form words. "How could you mislead that sweet woman at the desk?"

"I didn't." He nuzzled the pulse that throbbed at her temple. "We met one week ago. I *am* an honest man," he declared as he nibbled her cheek.

"You really are a crazy man."

"Mmm, about you," he murmured against her throat as he set about proving it.

With little effort, he aroused the primal woman beneath her facade. She'd denied all week that there was anything between them, but the denial had grown weaker with each day, until finally she'd admitted to herself and to him that she wanted him. From a beginning that had started with a kiss that had shaken her to her very toes, a magical fire had been laid. The embers had been fanned, and tonight the flame burned bright, consuming every argument she'd had against falling in love with this man. Expressing that love in the most intimate and profound way was right and exactly what she wanted.

Guided by Lynda's hands, Kent unsnapped the fastening at her waist, and seconds later the teal silk lay in a shimmering pool at her feet. His jacket and tie followed. Her slip. His shoes were kicked aside, then hers. With each garment that was taken off their bodies, they moved closer to the high four-poster bed that dominated the room.

Bathed in the light from a small bedside lamp, they stood naked, faced with the beauty of each other's bodies. "I was wrong last week," Kent whispered reverently. With shaking hands, he cupped her breasts. "This doesn't make us even. I'm getting the better present, and it's not even my birthday yet."

His words were a reminder of his parting shot that first day. Then, she'd considered them a dare, one she'd had no idea of ever taking up. But now they seemed a request, and she thrilled in the granting.

Under his heated gaze, she felt beautiful, an equal to his male perfection. Lynda gasped in exquisite agony when he lowered his head to her breasts. He caught one nipple between his lips and caressed it with his tongue while his fingers adored the surrounding flesh. Pleasure warmed and weakened her, but before her legs gave way completely, he laid her down on the bed, then lay down beside her, his weight dipping the mattress slightly so that her body slid across the sheets to meet his.

"You are so very beautiful," he murmured as he clasped her chin with his fingers and studied her face. "I promise I'll make you glad you let me love you."

Love you. The words matched the promise he was making to her with his eyes. She wanted to say those words, openly declare to him and to herself what she'd concluded the evening before, but she couldn't, not yet, maybe not ever. Making love and loving could be two different things.

She already knew she was a fool for letting him into her heart. She would be twice the fool, now, if she laid that heart out totally unprotected. Declarations of love were usually followed by promises of commitment, and Kent wasn't the kind of man to want those. Even if he did, she couldn't commit herself to a man like him. This was an affair, and whether it was brief or long, she would love this man with her body without saying the words.

"I'm already glad," she said, curving her hand to his cheek. Lifting her head, she pressed her lips softly to his, beginning the telling she could not put into words. Having been tantalized by his body that first day, teased further with each embrace they'd shared since, she couldn't wait to explore all its beauty. Her fingers journeyed over the sleek lines of his torso, feathering strokes that made every sinew and muscle shift and ripple beneath her fingertips.

When she slid her palm over the taut, smooth flesh below his navel, she felt his muscles contract, and she thrilled with knowledge that her touch could incite him so effectively. Emboldened, she slid her fingers lower. He groaned and grasped her hand.

"Far too uneven if you keep that up," Kent muttered thickly. "My turn."

Letting go of her hand, he started his own exploration. He savored her soft skin with his fingers, then his mouth, wanting to trace every delectable inch of her with his lips and tongue.

Sweeping his hands to her silken thighs, he caressed her until she was writhing beneath him. Applying the pressure of his hand to the heated spot, he soothed her momentarily. He slid back up her body and took her mouth as he never had before.

He swept his tongue inside her with a hot, hungry penetration that set an urgency within her that she'd never known. While his tongue moved in rhythmic thrusts, his fingers stoked the fires of her need until she was clutching him in frantic need.

"Oh, Kent," she moaned, needing him to become a part of her. Feeling him shift between her thighs and poise above her, she waited impatiently until he was prepared then arched her body to meet him.

Kent sank into her softness, crying her name as he felt her melt and flow around him. He moved slowly at first, murmuring words of no meaning, and Lynda answered with the same. Yet, each knew the sounds were those of pleasure given and taken. They fit perfectly together, as they moved in a slow, sweet dance of perfection that denied this was the first time for their loving.

Kent wanted to prolong this time, to fulfill his promise that she would be glad for having given into the magic he'd guessed their loving would be. But his control was taxed when she sought to increase their closeness and pressed her hands over his buttocks, taking him fully inside her. He held that position only briefly before the magic that had settled over both of them from the start completely took over. Their bodies drove harder and faster toward the ultimate peak, a fulfillment of such ecstasy neither wanted to leave it.

Long, sweet moments later, when they at last lay spent in each other's arms, Kent was first to attempt speech. "I'll never be able to play 'Dreamsville' in public again," he said haltingly, still attempting to bring his breathing to normal.

"But it's my favorite." Lynda's voice was no more steady than Kent's, and she hadn't the strength to question his statement. "You play it so wonderfully."

"For you," he clarified. "For you alone, from now on."

Propping himself up with one elbow, he gazed down at her. Her lips were moist, her breasts were flushed from his possession, and her eyes were two dark, deep pools reflecting his face. "What just happened was even better than I'd dreamed." He kissed the tip of her nose. "We went to 'Dreamsville.'"

"Mmm." Lynda sighed blissfully. She couldn't agree more, nor could she have described their loving in better terms, except that what had just happened went way beyond dreams.

"That's why I've been dedicating that piece to you, you know."

"I'd wondered."

"Afraid to ask?"

"You never gave me the chance," she answered, thinking of their silent walks to the waiting taxi and the nightly embraces that had been their way of saying good-night.

She felt rather than heard his response, a smile of satisfaction. Under other circumstances she might have challenged that satisfaction, but not tonight. Not at this moment, lying sated in each other's arms, enjoying the afterglow of their lovemaking.

Kent shifted to his back, pulling her over him. Combing his fingers through her hair, he tugged lightly on the golden strands to bring her face down to his. "You are a dream," he said, before kissing her gently, then tucking her head against his shoulder.

Sighing contentedly, he pressed his lips to her forehead. "'Dreamsville,'" he murmured against her flesh while his hands made circular patterns on her back. He concentrated on slowing his breathing, but already he could feel his body reawakening.

So could Lynda. Startled, but delighted, she raised her head. "Take me there again," she whispered, and put her mouth over his.

Kent made a garbled sound in his throat, but it wasn't a protest. He reached for her hips, lifted her, then eased her downward until again he was captured in her warmth. To her astonishment, she, who, in her inexperience, had begun to believe the labels—prude, frigid, too proper—discovered the sensual woman within her that Kent had always believed existed.

Minutes or hours passed, Lynda didn't know which, for time had no meaning or relevancy. All that was real or relevant was the surge of Kent's body and the answering flow of her own as they came together again and again.

In the twilight of semiconsciousness before true wakefulness, Lynda took a deep breath, then let it out slowly. Yawning, she stretched. That's when she came fully awake.

Her leg had slid along another, and her foot now rested on another. She felt a heavy arm wrapped around her middle. Startled, she froze for a moment, then relaxed. Kent.

Sometime in the hours just before dawn, they'd fallen asleep, nestled together like spoons. Lying very still, she listened to Kent's steady breathing and knew he was still fast asleep.

She felt the heat of a flush spread over her entire body when she thought of why the man was sleeping so deeply. He was exhausted. Considering the night they'd shared, so should she be, but she guessed the inner clock that had awakened her promptly at seven all her life had done its usual effective job.

She was awake but had no desire to leap immediately out of bed—her habit. Her mind had awakened, but her body had different ideas. She felt languid, filled with a heavy lassitude that made her wonder if she'd ever rise. Thinking she might convince her mind to return to sleep, she snuggled her body a little deeper into the warm embrace of the man fitted to her back.

This was a first, a wonderful first. She'd never spent an entire night with a man nor awakened in a man's arms. It was a wonderful experience, she decided, when the man was the man you loved.

Contented and secure in his embrace, she closed her eyes and strove for sleep. It wouldn't come. Her eyes shot open, and her body stiffened. She'd just spent the night with Kent, which meant she hadn't gone home, which meant that Suzanne must be frantic with worry by now. What had seemed a wonderful first moments before now seemed a supreme example of selfish irresponsibility.

Lynda sat up and looked at the small table beside the bed. No telephone. Frantically, she looked around the room. A wash stand complete with porcelain bowl and pitcher stood between a pair of windows. A large armoire occupied most of another wall.

Charming, she fumed, glaring at the furniture that was either antique or very well-done reproductions.

The room's decor was authentic nineteenth century down to the finest detail. Under other circumstances she would have been delighted with it. Instead, as her eyes swept the room again, she prayed that the proprietors hadn't carried the replication of a bygone time to such an extreme that no telephones were available in the guest rooms. Finally, she spied the phone sitting on a small table at the far corner of the room.

Tossing back the covers, she started to get out of bed. Just as quickly, she pulled the covers back over her. She was totally nude. That state hadn't bothered her a bit the night before, but in the clear light of the morning sun beginning to brighten the room, she felt suddenly far too vulnerable.

She grabbed the comforter and wrapping it around herself, she started out of bed again, when she heard, "Going somewhere?"

Startled, she looked back, clutching the comforter protectively in front of her. "You're awake!"

Propped on one elbow, Kent growled, "Pretty hard not to be with you leaping in and out of bed. What's the emergency?"

"I have to call Suzanne and let her know I'm okay," Lynda said as she backed farther away from the bed. "She'll be worried sick by now. She's probably called every hospital in Franklin County, plus the state highway patrol."

"Why?"

"Why? Isn't it obvious?" Lynda snapped, reaching for the telephone. "I didn't come home last night, and she was expecting me."

"No, she wasn't."

"You don't know my sister," Lynda stated as she studied the directions on how to make a long-distance call. "We always let each other know where we're going and when we're likely to be home."

"A wise and courteous thing to do," Kent stated, surprising her.

"Glad you finally understand," she muttered sarcastically as she began to dial. Obviously, Kent lived alone. His comings and goings were no doubt his own business and had been so for so long that he'd forgotten what being responsible to someone else entailed— if that sense of responsibility had ever been instilled in him.

"Put down the phone," he ordered. "It's not necessary." She started to tell him exactly how necessary it was, but he countered with, "Suzanne knew you were with me."

"But I didn't...how could she know?" Undaunted by his order, Lynda started to dial until the implication of his last statement dawned on her. "She knew?" she asked suspiciously. "What did you do, call her up yesterday and say, 'By the way, I'm planning on seducing your sister tonight, so don't expect her home?'"

"No, I had lunch with Jay and mentioned I had reservations here. Since he was planning on seeing your sister last night, I asked him to relay the information."

"You told Jay? Why didn't you take out an ad in the *Columbus Dispatch*?" Fury mixed with humiliation. "How could you!"

Kent chuckled, then quickly apologized for making fun of her concern. "Relax, sweetheart. All I said was that I was taking you to the Granville Inn and to let Suzanne know you were with me and where we were. Your sister has no doubt figured out why you weren't

home last night and is thinking nothing more than
what a good little matchmaker she is.''

Lynda wasn't particularly appeased by his speech
but she was no longer worried that her sister feared
she'd been mugged or kidnapped. However, she
wasn't at all comforted by the knowledge that Suzanne knew where she'd been all night and what she'd
been doing. She blushed again.

Guessing at the reason for the color that painted
Lynda's cheeks, Kent felt a surge of tenderness he'd
never experienced before. Unconcerned with his nudity, he swung himself out of bed and in two strides
was beside Lynda. Wrapping his arms around her, he
pulled her close.

"I'll pound the first person who even thinks about
making anything tawdry out of last night," he promised. "Including you." He picked her up, comforter
and all, and sat down in the chair next to the phone.
Tucking her head beneath his chin, he stated, "What
we did together last night was beautiful, and I won't
allow you to have any regrets."

His tenderness and understanding were blurring her
embarrassment and softening her fury. Still, she felt
compelled to challenge his high-handed order. "How
do you expect to prevent me?"

"By taking you back to bed and spending the rest of
the weekend loving you so thoroughly, you'll be too
occupied to think of anything but me."

Lynda jerked upright. "That is the most egotistical
statement you've ever made, and you've made some
whoppers!"

He caught her chin with his fingers and grinned at her. "Just a statement of fact, my love," he said and promptly smothered her astonishment with a kiss that was the first step in the validation of his statement.

Ten

___

Seated across the linen-draped table from her brother, a teasing twinkle in her eyes, Theresa casually commented, "According to my sources, you've been seeing quite a lot of a certain optometrist."

"Your sources are correct," Kent replied, carefully schooling his features to reveal nothing but great interest in the noontime offerings at the Columbus Club. It didn't take a genius to know where Theresa was going to lead this conversation, if he let her. She wanted to know exactly how successful her matchmaking effort had been, and for the life of him, he really didn't know the answer. Until this morning, he would have said very successful. In light of what had happened at Lynda's office when he'd picked up his new glasses, he was beginning to have his doubts.

Doubt was a mild word for what he was feeling about his relationship with Lynda. Shock, rejection, fury were more apt. Two hours ago, while dispensing his glasses, Lynda had informed him that she could not have dinner with him tonight. That had been a disappointment, but he had handled it. However, when he'd asked about tomorrow night, she'd firmly said no, then repeated the answer in response to another invitation.

If all that hadn't been bad enough, she'd gone on to inform him, in no uncertain terms, that Saturday night was all she could ''afford'' to spend with him for the rest of this week—and every week here on. This from the woman he was about to ask to marry him! He should have known better than to ask. She always balked, and this morning she'd been a rock.

In a barely controlled rage, he'd stormed out. At his own office, he'd uncharacteristically snapped at the receptionist, then his own secretary, and he'd snarled at one of the messengers. The blanched expression on the kid's normally sunny face had brought Kent up short, and he'd quickly apologized, then gone about smoothing the ruffled feathers of the rest of the staff. After that, he'd closed his door and brooded in private until his luncheon date with Theresa.

Patience never having been one of her strong suits, Kent saw that she wanted to smack the table in frustration at his brief answer. In an attempt to prompt further information out of him, Theresa teased, ''Having some problem with your eyes or something?''

''Not any more.'' His answer brought a gasp of exasperation from her. Not the answer you expected, little sister? he asked silently. Not mine, either, he thought, grimly wondering if his three simple words marked the end of more than his eye strain. He reached into the pocket of his suit jacket and extracted his brand-new pair of reading glasses. Slipping them on, he commented, "Mmm...much better."

"You're wearing glasses!" Theresa's statement of the obvious made Kent smile slightly.

"How astute of you to point that out," Kent retorted, earning him another gasp of exasperation.

"So you have a vision problem?" Theresa asked, dumbfounded.

"I did until I got these," was his nonchalant comment as he continued to study the menu. No problem with my vision, just my vision expert, he thought. "I'm having the bluefish. What about you?"

Theresa's answer was a killing glare and the rapid drumming of her perfect manicured fingertips on the table top, mannerisms so typical of their mother's means of showing both impatience and disapproval that Kent would have laughed if he hadn't been so miserable.

The waiter's arrival for their order saved Kent further cross-examination, but only temporarily, for as soon as the young man had left, Theresa exploded. "Nobody sees their optometrist nightly and spends the weekend with him just because he needs glasses!"

"I certainly wouldn't—if my optometrist were a *him*," Kent replied with forced calm. Inside he was questioning if he was ever going to see his optometrist again on anything but a professional basis.

Theresa sent him a narrow-eyed glare. "Cute, Kent. Real cute. Now that you've had your fun, what's happening with you and Lynda? You saw her every night last week and spent the weekend with her. This is only Wednesday, but the pattern seems to be repeating itself, except that you're not playing at the club and so you're taking her elsewhere for dinner and—" she waggled her eyebrows "—whatever, till the wee hours each night. To my knowledge, you've never spent that much steady time with any one woman. Could it be this one's special, very special?"

"Do you have a detective following me or something?" Kent demanded irritatedly. "If you do, he's not doing a very good job."

"My informant is doing a very good job," Theresa declared haughtily to Kent's growling tone. "After all, she lives with her. Suzanne certainly knows when and if her sister comes home each night."

"No, she doesn't," Kent refuted, though he was confused. "I've been with Lynda all of those times, but I have not kept her out till the wee hours as you so quaintly put it. I've had her back in the parking lot behind her office by ten every night this week, the same as last week."

Theresa was obviously undaunted by his black scowl. "Well, according to Suzanne, Lynda's not coming home until long after midnight."

Where in blue blazes had Lynda been for hours after he dropped her off at her office? And with whom? No wonder she'd looked pale and drawn this morning. It had to be exhausting carrying on such a busy social life!

When I get my hands on the second-shift sleaze-ball— As soon as the image of a featureless male being strangled formed in Kent's mind, another image appeared. Lynda's wounded face. The way she'd looked when he'd unwittingly accused her of reacting to other men's kisses the way she reacted to his.

There was no other man in her life as surely as there was no other woman in his. Lynda was a one-man kind of woman, and he'd become a one-woman kind of man.

She was everything he wanted in a woman. He was sure he was everything she wanted in a man. He was positive that she had fallen as deeply in love as he had. But she'd fallen in love with the wrong man. She even knew that. What she didn't know was that the wrong man was the right man, a man she didn't know, not entirely.

"There is no other man," he stated firmly, his black mood lightened considerably.

"I'm sure there isn't," Theresa quickly agreed.

"Well, there is, but it's high time he was done away with," he said, throwing his sister into obvious total confusion.

Tossing his napkin on the table, he pushed his chair back. "Sorry, Theresa, but I can't stay for lunch," he said as he rose and motioned for their waiter. He quickly advised the young man to put the two lunches on his tab.

"Please don't do anything rash, Kent," Theresa pleaded. Just before Kent fled the distinguished dining room, she promised, "I'll never do anything like this again, Kent."

* * *

A long, narrow white florist's box tucked under one arm, his briefcase under the other and a wicker picnic hamper swinging from one hand, Kent knocked lightly on the door to Lynda's office. Whistling softly to himself, he waited for it to open. Seconds turned to minutes that seemed like hours. "Come on, sweetheart, I know you're in there," he muttered as he waited. "Your car's still parked out behind the building."

Receiving no answer, he rapped again, a bit more loudly and a bit more impatiently. His whistling grew louder.

Lynda, standing on the other side of the door, could almost recognize the tune. "Go away, you crazy, irresistible man." Lynda whispered the words so softly, they were barely discernible to her own ears. "I can't afford time with you. I really do have work to do."

She'd taken the precaution of locking the door as soon as the last of the staff had gone for the day. Kent had left in a huff that morning, but she hadn't really believed that her edict that Saturdays were all she could afford to give him was going to stop him from showing up as usual. Kent Berringer didn't understand the meaning of the word *no*. He'd proved that over and over.

When six o'clock had come and gone, she'd almost believed he'd accepted her pronouncement. Telling herself that she wasn't at all disappointed, she'd tackled composing some letters. Deep in concentration, the soft tap on the office door at seven had startled her, but she'd guessed immediately who the caller was.

She'd practically run to the door to let him in, then pulled herself up short at the last possible second.

Every word she'd said that morning had been absolutely true. She didn't have time for an intense relationship with a man, and the sooner she put a stop to their daily meetings the better. Despite her determination to have only a meaningless affair with him, she had fallen in love. Seeing him daily was only strengthening her feelings, feelings that would ultimately lead to destruction. Her relationship with Kent Berringer had to stop. She was prepared to go cold turkey if necessary.

The whistling stopped, and Lynda leaned closer to the door, hoping to hear retreating footsteps. Nothing. She leaned even closer to make sure.

She heard sounds, but not footsteps. A soft thud and a light, almost musical tinkling. And then another soft thud. After a minute or two, she heard what sounded like paper tearing. A second later, a folded piece of lined yellow paper slid under the door.

Lynda stared down at it. She wanted to ignore it, but curiosity forced her to bend down and pick it up. With shaking fingers, she unfolded the paper, wondering fleetingly why he'd have a sheet of legal yellow paper handy.

Lynda,
Please let me in so I can apologize properly. I'm an insensitive jerk, but I promise to change my ways, starting tonight. When you let me in, I'll explain why I understand.

Kent

P.S. I'm prepared to camp out in the hallway.

"You would, wouldn't you?" she said aloud.

"Damned right!" The response echoed from the hallway.

Lynda unlocked the door and swung it open. All her good intentions and rationalizations for cutting Kent out of her life warred with her emotions as she took in the sight of him. Within seconds, her dreary mood lifted and her body warmed. And, as always, any thought of resisting the dictates of her heart fled.

Having decided he was in for a long wait, Kent was seated on the floor of the hallway. He sprang agilely to his feet with the simple apology, "I'm sorry."

Involuntarily, she glided toward the embrace of his strong arms. "I'm sorry, too. I wasn't thinking straight this morning," she blurted.

"Neither was I," he said. He took her lips in a tender kiss that told her more profoundly than words how sorry he was that they'd argued that morning.

"Oh, what am I going to do about you?" Lynda complained softly when she could form words.

"Exactly as you're doing would be just fine," Kent told her. Wrapping her more tightly against him, he kissed her again.

"What is it that you understand?" she asked when he finally released her.

"That you have work to do," he said, picking up the hamper, florist box and his briefcase. "Can we go inside, or do you want to continue carrying on in the hallway?"

"Inside," she answered, and stepped out of the doorway so that he could enter. Though she'd gone willingly into his arms a moment before, skepticism was rearing its head again. "Why should I believe that you suddenly understand that I really do need to work? Why the sudden turnaround?''

"Because I suddenly put myself in your place with a reminder that I've had weeks like this myself. Contrary to what you've been led to believe about me, I really do work, daily, even." His declaration brought a look of confusion to Lynda's features. Not surprised by her reaction, he smiled and handed her the florist box.

"Explanations will come in due time," he promised, and kissed the tip of her nose. "But first, a proper apology for being an insensitive jerk."

Somewhat mollified, Lynda slipped the ribbon from the box and lifted the lid. Inside lay a dozen deep red roses. Touching one of the velvety petals, she blinked back tears. "Oh, Kent, they're beautiful, but I don't deserve them. I really snapped at you this morning. When you brought up going out tonight, all I could think about was the mountain of paperwork on my desk."

"The mountain that's beckoned you in here every night after I brought you back to the parking lot?" In response to her look of surprise, he said, "I had a little chat with your receptionist this afternoon. She told me all about how late you've been staying, the extra responsibilities you've taken onto yourself because of Dr. Kelsey's illness and how tired you've been all week."

Lynda's eyes widened farther, and Kent took the box of roses from her, then guided her to a chair. "Now comes the explaining part. I've had times when I've had to stay late at my office. Believe me, I do understand that no profession is a nine-to-five job. My profession's the same.''

"Your office?" she asked dumbly. "Your profession?"

"My profession," he confirmed. "My office is downtown in the Huntington Building. I'm an attorney by day, and I play a mean trombone at night, but only when the other guys and I have time. They've got other jobs, too. We had dreams of stardom when we were kids, but wised up after a while and got our educations and succeeded in establishing ourselves in more dependable careers than music. These days, getting together and playing a gig every so often is more or less a hobby.''

He was busy spreading a cloth on the floor and setting up the dinners he'd packed into the hamper, so Lynda was sure he didn't see the clouds that were surely gathering on her face. Almost from the beginning, she'd suspected that there was far more to Kent than he was telling her. These revelations were perfect solutions to all the riddles about the man, save one. Why had he kept all of this a secret until now? Especially since the truth would have saved a lot of misunderstandings.

Uncomfortably aware that he was babbling, Kent continued on anyway. This wasn't at all the way he'd planned to make a clean breast of things with her. Having put it off so long, he found no easy way of doing it. Blurting it all out quickly seemed the only option.

"What I have here is the necessary nourishment for two hardworking professionals who need to catch up on the paperwork they've been neglecting while they've been pursuing a meaningful relationship. Come, Doctor, let's eat," he invited expansively. Reaching for her hand, he tugged gently to urge her down to the floor.

Jerking her hand away, Lynda strode to the farthermost corner of the room. "Stay over there," she warned when he started for her. "Don't you touch me, you... you... Just who are you?"

Golden fire leaped from her large eyes, which moments before had been soft pools reflecting all the love he was feeling for her. The mouth that had been soft and giving beneath his was drawn in a tight line. He was in deep trouble, and he cursed himself for playing such a damn fool game with her.

"I just explained who I am," he started carefully. "You can look in the yellow pages under 'attorneys' and find my name listed. And since I'm making a clean breast of things, I'm not rich by Rockefeller standards, but I'm more than comfortable. My law practice is healthy, and that stuffy family I told you about are the founders and controllers of Capital City Bank. That's supposed to make us Berringers one of *the* families of Columbus."

Shock widened her eyes. Her throat felt tight. A feeling that she'd been made a fool of chilled her body. "Why didn't you tell me before now?" she demanded in a whisper.

"It just never came up," he offered, feeling as if he were tied up and the knot was getting a bit tighter. He'd thought a quick confession would dissolve that bind, but it had only made it worse.

Defensive anger replaced her shock, and Lynda went on the offense. "That is no excuse!" Advancing on him, she accused, "You could have told me almost any time. Right after you cleared up the stripper business would have been appropriate."

"You were pretty busy plotting revenge, and I was busy trying to figure out a way to get you interested in me for more reasons than the number of dollars in my bank account," he offered. His reasons for playing a role had made sense at the beginning. They were looking pretty foolish now. A quick glance at Lynda told him she wasn't softening at all. If anything, she was becoming more furious.

"I'll admit I let the charade go on too long," he said quickly. "And I'm sorry for that. It was stupid."

Lynda neither acknowledged the apology nor refuted his statement. Rigid, she continued to glare at him.

Feeling more and more uneasy, he suggested, "I suppose I could have paused last weekend and said, 'Oh, by the way, darling, not only am I not a professional male stripper, but I'm not a professional musician, either. I'm an attorney.' I don't think you would have believed me."

Lifting a censorious brow, Lynda snapped, "I might have."

"Sure you would have," he drawled with a grin, trying to defuse her anger. "About as much as Lois Lane might have believed Clark Kent telling her he was Superman right after he'd tripped over his own feet."

Lynda softened her stance only slightly. "Okay, you could be right about that, but you still should have told me sometime before now. We didn't spend all last weekend in bed. We did a lot of talking. During any one of those times you could have told me what you do for a living. Or over dinner anytime last week. That would have been infinitely better than waiting until now."

"You're right," Kent admitted. "I should have, but if I had, would it have made any difference in the way you feel about me?"

"I sure would have had fewer reservations about getting involved with you!" she stated quickly and angrily.

Her response pricked one of his sore spots. "So, Kent Berringer, rich attorney, is more acceptable to Dr. Lynda Fisher than Kent Berringer, lowly local musician? Is money and prestige that important to you?"

"Yes!" she answered without thinking, then quickly amended, "I mean, no!"

"Which is it, Lynda?" Kent sneered, covering the pain he was feeling with anger. He had been wrong about her. Turning the tables, he advanced on her. "I've got plenty of both," he snarled. "If they're what really turns you on."

"Stop it!" she screamed. His words felt like blows on her body. "You don't understand! Someone like you could never understand!"

"Oh, I understand," he roared back, too caught up in his own hurt to see hers. "That old family wealth means instant acceptance to people like you!"

"To some people, maybe," she cried. "Stupid, weak, foolish people who don't know how to live any other way. Old family wealth doesn't turn me on, as you so crudely put it. You can't depend on it. Easy money, money you didn't work for yourself, can be snatched away from you just like your home can be snatched away from you.'' The disappointments and fears of her childhood spurred her into a rambling, disjointed, near-hysterical tale of things and people being snatched away from her.

At first Kent could make little sense of what she was saying except that somehow he sensed it was important not to stop her. He listened in growing horror as she described a childhood that seesawed from wealth to abject poverty.

''We couldn't live in the house anymore because Papa's business had gone bankrupt again and there wasn't any money left. The bus station was awful, but Suzanne and I had to stay there until Papa came back for us. He promised it wouldn't be very long, but it was days. I tried not to cry because Suzanne was so scared and I had to protect her because Mama wasn't there anymore. I was twelve, a big girl, Papa's dependable one, and I could keep Suzanne safe. I've always kept Suzanne safe.''

Kent shuddered at the image of a frightened twelve-year-old huddling in a bus station with only her little sister for company. She'd pledged to keep her little sister safe, but who had kept her safe?

When he saw her begin to crumple, he was across the room in one stride, pulling her into his arms, absorbing her heavy sobbing against the strength of his chest. ''Sweetheart, sweetheart,'' he crooned. ''You're safe, now. You'll always be safe.'' His voice was not too steady as he soothed her. The image of a frightened little girl with big brown eyes hurt him as much as that little girl had been hurt.

''I thought you were like him,'' Lynda snuffled against Kent's shirt.

"Like who, sweetheart?" he asked softly, burying his lips into her hair.

As if a dam had burst, Lynda's words tumbled out. "Papa," she said simply, before explaining everything about her father, his wealthy upbringing and the shock of losing it all with unwise investments, his flamboyant ways, his irresponsibility. "Always a new scheme, a rainbow just around the corner, and we always believed him. All that we could ever depend on was Papa saying that everything would get better. Oh, how we trusted him."

Kent listened, not interrupting her as the rest of the story came out. At some point, still holding her close, he managed to get them both to the double settee, where he cradled her on his lap and she snuggled her head beneath his chin. He held her and stroked her back while she talked.

When she stopped talking, he continued to hold her and soothe the quiet sobs that still wracked through her slender body.

He'd misjudged her, all right, but not in the way he'd first thought. Her abhorrence of play, her workaholic habits, her concern for professional image, all of it made sense. And it all proved without a doubt that he was exactly the kind of man she needed. Not the guy he'd invented to prove a point with her, though she needed a good dose of him, too, but the real Kent Berringer, every side of him.

And he needed her, wanted her, loved her. But she wasn't ready to hear about that yet. She needed some time, time to come to grips with the whole man.

"The crazy thing is, I know he really did love us, and I never stopped loving him, even when he let us down time and time again," Lynda said when she'd recovered. "And you came along and seemed to be a reincarnation of him and just as irresistible."

"Irresistible, am I?" Kent teased lightly, sensing that the storm was over and the mood needed to be changed.

Lynda lifted her head from the comforting pillow of his shoulder and smiled. "You know you are, you egotist."

He was hard put to keep from asking if it followed that she also might love him, but he managed to refrain. Now wasn't the time, he reminded himself. Instead, he said, "You're pretty irresistible yourself, you know."

Kissing the tip of her nose, he gently set her away from him. "But I promised to change my ways, and I'm going to keep that promise and prove what an honest, trustworthy guy I am."

"Still trying to convince me you were an Eagle Scout?" Lynda teased.

"I was," he declared. "I'll show you the badge and certificate this weekend when I take you to my place."

"Your place?"

"My place," he confirmed with a nod. "You're forewarned, but I'm not taking a no from you. I only told you so you can tell your sister where you'll be Saturday evening, Saturday night and most of Sunday. I understand responsibility to others. Right now I have a responsibility to you. Instead of pulling you down on the floor and spending the rest of the evening making passionate love to you, I'm going to feed you instead. Then I'm going to march you into your office back there and let you work for a couple of hours while I do the same out here. And then I'm going to escort you to your car and follow you home, to make sure you get a decent night's sleep."

He brushed his thumbs lightly across her cheeks. "You, my love, need someone to take care of you. You've got to learn how to budget your time, get your priorities in order."

Lynda began to laugh. "Get my priorities in order? This from the man who for the last week and a half has been doing everything possible to mix them up?"

"That was that other guy, the one I pretend to be when the emotional baggage of my own life gets too heavy," he said as he guided her down to the picnic he'd spread out on the floor. "I'll tell you about him sometime, but we've had enough confessions for one night, don't you think?"

Feeling emotionally drained, Lynda had to agree with Kent. Still, she was reluctant to keep any more secrets between them. "I suppose so, but you promise to tell me about him? Soon?"

"Scout's honor," Kent pledged, handing her a plate.

"Some Scout you are," Lynda grumbled. "You've been lying to me ever since I met you."

"No, I haven't" he defended. "Everything I told you about myself is true."

"You just left out some rather important parts."

"Well, now you know them all except one."

"And what is that?"

"I'll tell you Saturday night, right after I show you my Eagle badge. I promise. Now quit wasting time with all this talk and eat, so we can get some work done. I've got a brief to prepare for a hearing tomorrow, and good attorneys are like good Boy Scouts. They're always prepared.''

Eleven

In disbelief, Lynda stared at the framed ribboned badge with the dangling silver eagle that held a place of honor on the wall of Kent's den. "You weren't kidding. You really were an Eagle Scout."

"You've got to start believing me," Kent said, sliding an arm around her waist. "I am an honest man who keeps his promises."

"Always?" she questioned lightly, still having trouble believing everything Kent had told her about himself.

"Haven't I been proving that all week?" he asked, turning her in his arms. "I promised I'd make sure you had plenty of time to get your work done, and I have. I've brought you nourishment so you'd have enough strength to plow through all that paperwork, and then I've escorted you home so that you'd get a good night's rest, so that you could do your very best the next day. I'd say I deserve some sort of reward for such good behavior.''

Sliding her hands up his chest and locking them behind his head, she reached up on her toes and kissed him. "How's that?''

"It's a start.''

Pulling his head down, she kissed him again, lingering longer, tracing the outline of his lips with the tip of her tongue before she released him. "How about that?''

"Better." Wrapping his arms around her, he lowered his mouth to hers and delivered the kind of kiss that was his specialty. The kind that weakened her knees, raised her blood pressure and rendered her mind totally useless.

When she could speak again, she murmured, "Whose reward was that?''

"Ours. I don't know about you, but I've been going absolutely crazy all week keeping my hands off of you.''

His hands weren't staying off of her now. His fingers made short work of the buttons on her blouse, slid the garment away from her and flipped it toward the wing chair that occupied one corner of the small, cozy den. Curling his palms over her arms, he ran them up and down the length before smoothing over her back. "You have the softest, silkiest skin in the world," he murmured as he lowered his lips to her shoulder. "And you taste fantastic.''

Lynda arched her neck, giving him easier access to her throat. Her hands weren't idle, either; though slower than his, they were making steady progress at removing his shirt. She was as anxious to touch him as he was to touch her.

She'd appreciated his trustworthiness about working every evening. Under his consistent proctoring, she'd made steady progress in the mountain of paperwork. Today, a mere hour after the last patient, Lynda had left the office, her desk completely clear for the first time since Dr. Kelsey's heart attack.

But there had been moments when she would have been absolutely delighted if Kent had broken his promise. Working at her desk in her private office and knowing Kent was but a few feet away at the receptionist's desk hadn't been conducive to concentration. Gradually it had become easier, and by weeks' end they'd established a satisfying routine.

"Speaking of promises..." Lynda paused as she pressed light kisses across his chest. "Wasn't there something else you wanted to tell me about yourself. I've seen your Eagle badge," she prompted.

Kent stilled the hands that had been about to remove her linen slacks. He cradled her face and looked long into her eyes. They were soft and wide, reflecting his image in their warm brown depths and, he hoped, what was in his heart. "I love you, Lynda."

Of all the possible revelations that had teased her curiosity, that he loved her had never occurred to her. Though he'd made some reference to a meaningful relationship, she'd not expected it to be this meaningful. Even with all he'd told her about himself Wednesday evening, she hadn't expected him to be the kind of man who'd want anything but an affair. "You love me? Why?"

He smiled and shook his head slowly, as if he were as amazed at the revelation as she was. "God only knows, since you've been so intent on proving I'm the wrong man for you. I guess I worked so hard proving that assessment erroneous that I also proved to myself that you're the right woman for me."

"The right woman for you?" she asked dumbly.

Kent chuckled. "Is there an echo in this room?" he teased lightly. "Yes, my love, the right woman for me. Last weekend gave me a taste of what sharing every night and waking up every morning with you would be like. This week, working in the evenings together, I've gotten another sample of what sharing our lives could be like. And I want that to continue next week, every week. I want to marry you, Lynda Fisher. The sooner, the better."

Lynda couldn't form an answer. She loved him and should be overjoyed that he'd just declared his love for her, backing it up with a proposal of marriage. It was all too wonderful. He was too wonderful. She froze, and all the old protective devices she'd developed to deal with disappointments fell into place.

In response to her unblinking, wide-eyed stare, Kent prodded, "A simple yes will do."

Lynda swallowed hard, forcing down the lump that threatened to close up her throat entirely. "I can't," she said, her tone flat and lifeless.

Kent frowned and dropped his hands from her face. He'd braced himself for an immediate no, declared vehemently. He was used to those from her and knew he could turn one into a yes quite easily. But an "I can't?" One spoken quietly and slowly, with no emotion? He couldn't believe what he was hearing.

Trying for patience, he asked, "Do you love me, Lynda?"

Blinking back tears, she didn't want to look at him, but his tone, deep and gentle, compelled her to meet his eyes. She was immediately caught by those wondrous blue depths that had been hypnotizing her for two weeks now. "Yes, I love you. But I won't marry you. I can't."

Kent's head jerked back as if she'd struck him. "Let me get this straight. You love me but for some reason you can't marry me. Got a husband tucked away somewhere? Because that's the only reason I can imagine that would keep you from saying yes."

Suddenly very conscious of the nudity of her upper body, Lynda moved away from him and picked up her blouse from the chair. Holding it in front of her like a shield, she said, "There are other reasons."

Shoving his hands into his pants pockets to keep from reaching for her, he asked, "Like what?"

Not fully knowing the reasons herself, except for the overwhelming sense of fear that had come over her, Lynda grasped at the first thing she could think of. "You lied to me."

"Try again," he fired back. "We cleared that all up, and you damned well know it."

"Don't you swear at me."

"That wasn't swearing. If I was swearing at you, you'd hear a lot worse!"

Slipping her arms into her blouse, Lynda stated, "In the two weeks I've known you, you've never sworn."

"Well, I do upon occasion," he grumbled.

As soon as her blouse was buttoned, she tucked it into her slacks. Clothed, she felt far less vulnerable.

"That just proves how little we know each other. Two weeks just isn't enough time to fall in love and make plans to marry immediately."

"That's all it took to fall in love, but I suppose we can have a long engagement," he said, relaxing a little. "Just how long an engagement period do you need?"

"I didn't agree to marriage," Lynda said quickly, feeling as if she were being backed into a corner. "There's more to consider than time. Things I don't think you'd understand." How could he? she wondered. She didn't understand them herself.

His shirt still open and the tails still dangling free from his pants, Kent ambled over to the couch that filled one wall of the small room. "Try me," he said as he sat down. Smiling the thousand-watt smile that sent tiny bolts of lightning through her body, he patted the cushion beside him. "Come over here and sit down, and I'll show you just how understanding I can be."

Lynda took in his enticing pose. Was it unconscious, or was he using all his artillery? Seated on the couch, his perfect chest still exposed, one arm stretched over the back of the cushions, he invited her without words to snuggle up next to him. If she did, she wouldn't be able to resist him at all, and she would probably find herself married by morning. "Not on your life," she vowed, and promptly sat down on the chair close to the door.

"Okay, have it your way."

His tone had been nonchalant. His body was draped in a relaxed position, but Lynda didn't miss the intensity in his eyes or the flexing and unflexing of his fingers. He was as nervous as she was. Somehow, that knowledge made her feel better. This was no game he was playing, and he deserved honesty... if only she really knew what the honest answer was.

Crossing her legs, she folded her hands in her lap, trying not to grip them too tightly but enough to still their shaking. "I have the responsibility of my practice and Dr. Kelsey's since his heart attack."

"I thought he was back now," Kent inserted.

"He is, part-time. It'll be weeks before he's back full time. I can't desert him now."

"I wouldn't ask you to," Kent said. "Marrying me doesn't mean you're going to skip town. Have you noticed I live in this city, too? I have a practice of my own. I wouldn't desert it, so I certainly wouldn't ask you to desert yours. I'd like to take you on a nice long honeymoon, but it can wait until Kelsey's totally back on his feet. If we have to, we can even put off marrying until then."

He smiled at her, not the thousand watter, but the tender one that made her stomach flutter. "As I told you the other night, I do understand that no profession is a nine-to-five job. Now that we've shot down that excuse, got any more?"

He was being so accommodating, saying all the right things, and she was helpless to refute his reasoning. Inexplicably, fear gripped her more tightly. Her gaze raced frantically around the room as if she would find something to cling to, anything but the man who was asking her to share her life. "Suzanne," she blurted. "I can't abandon her. She depends on me, needs me."

Kent frowned, thinking of the laughing young woman who was Lynda's sister and fast becoming his sister's best friend. He knew Theresa had a soft heart, but she wasn't a collector of lost souls. Someone she chose as a friend would be as strong and independent as she. Nothing he knew or had seen about Suzanne indicated she was an exception. "Your sister's an adult," he stated firmly. "She doesn't need you."

"Oh, yes, she does! I can't abandon her."

His impatience clear in his tone, Kent argued, "She's not going to feel abandoned. She's not a child. Give your sister some credit. She doesn't need mothering anymore. From what I've seen, she's more than able to stand on her own two feet."

"But she can't, not entirely, not yet," Lynda cried, her voice rising with the panic growing within her. "She and the girls couldn't live without my financial support."

"Is that all you think she needs? If so, fine. I've got plenty of money. Turn all your earnings over to your sister for as long as she needs it or it makes you happy," Kent said, sensing that more than financial support of Lynda's sister and nieces was at the root of her refusal to marry him.

Feeling cold, shaky and terribly alone against an imaginary storm, Lynda wrapped her arms around her middle. "I knew you wouldn't understand," she asserted stubbornly, although she was unable to discount the feasibility of Kent's suggestion. "It isn't just money. You could never understand what it's been like for the two of us. She's been deserted by everybody else important to her. I can't just walk away from her."

"Can't or won't? What are you really afraid of, Lynda? That Suzanne will discover she really doesn't need you?" Rising from the couch, he advanced on her as he strengthened his attack. "Just who needs whom in your little family, Lynda?" he demanded.

"We need each other," Lynda declared, pushing herself up out of the chair. "She trusts me to be there for her. I can't betray that trust. She needs me."

Kent shook his head. "I don't think so, sweetheart. But you sure do need her to hide behind."

"I'm not hiding behind my sister!"

"What else would you call it?"

"Responsibility," she fired at him, and started through the doorway.

Kent was right on her heels, his hands back in his pockets to keep from physically halting her. "Running home to that safe little world you've built for yourself? What are you going to do when Suzanne flies from that nest? She will someday, you know. She's going to graduate soon, and that'll make a difference in her income. Maybe enough that she can afford a place of her own."

Lynda froze. Her thoughts went instantly back to the day Suzanne had brought up essentially the same thing. She whirled around and gave Kent the same response she'd given Suzanne. "She has a home."

"Who's making the payments on that home?"

"I am."

"Who buys the groceries, pays the utilities, the taxes?"

"I do."

"Then it's your home," he declared. "How old is Suzanne?"

"What does her age have to do with this?"

"Just answer the question," Kent demanded in courtroom fashion.

Beginning to feel as if she were a witness on the stand and had sworn to tell the whole truth and nothing but the truth, Lynda supplied, "Twenty-four."

"An adult," he said, stating the obvious, and Lynda frowned, wondering where this line of questioning was leading. She didn't have long to wonder, for his next question revealed the trap he'd led her into. "Isn't it the goal of a parent to ensure that when their children reach adulthood they're able to stand on their own two feet?"

"Well...yes, but..." Lynda hedged, feeling the trap closing tighter on her.

Not giving her a chance to finish, Kent fired a rapid series of questions at her. "And don't parents often make sure their children have an education so that they can support themselves? Make their own homes? Provide for their own children? Wouldn't you say a true adult wants those things? And a parent will know she's done a good job if her child not only has the ability to achieve those goals but the desire, as well? And have you not served as your sister's parent for the past ten years?"

He paused and smiled triumphantly as he asked one last question, "Would you say you've been a good parent?"

Suzanne's declaration that adult children had to make their own nests rang in Lynda's ears, and she admitted defeat. "Yes, I have. Suzanne wants and will soon be fully capable of being out on her own," she said flatly, accepting for the first time exactly what Suzanne had been trying to tell her for weeks.

"You should feel very proud of yourself for a job well done," Kent said. "Suzanne is a fine young woman."

"Yes, she is," Lynda agreed, but instead of feeling pride, she felt even more frightened. A sense of desperation came over her, and all she could think about was getting home and holding on tight to her family. "I'm going home."

"You'd better get there fast because it's going to be empty soon," he told her with cutting accuracy. "Is it going to be so safe and secure then?"

Lynda whirled around, "It'll always be safe. Nobody's ever lied to me in that world," she stated firmly. "It's built on love and trust."

"You don't know what that means! You're afraid to trust anybody but yourself," he said, then in exasperation he told her exactly what he thought of dredging up the excuse that he'd ever lied to her. He finished with an accusation that she was a liar for claiming to love him.

Refusing to dignify his accusation with a response, she kept on moving toward the elevator, praying her wait wouldn't be long. It wasn't; the doors opened a second after she hit the button. She was stepping into the elevator when she heard, "Come back here. I'll drive you home."

Remembering that she didn't have her car, she held the elevator open for a moment. The last thing she wanted to do was spend any more time in Kent Berringer's company. "I'll call my sister or a taxi. I don't need you."

She let go of the door and prayed it would close quickly. It didn't, and Kent held it open. Softly, he said, "No, I think you do need me."

"Goodbye, Kent," she stated with cold finality, and he released the door. The elevator door closed.

Fighting for composure, Lynda refused to give in to the tears that were threatening to fall. She held herself in stiff control as she stepped off the elevator and walked to a public phone in the lobby. She dialed her home number and waited through several rings before remembering that Suzanne was out with Jay. A baby-sitter was at the house with the girls. She hung up before there was an answer.

She was stranded, deserted. There was no one to come to her rescue. No one she could trust. She nearly screamed in panic when she felt a hand on her shoulder. It was Kent.

Before she could react, he put his arm around her waist and started toward the lobby doors. "Come on, I'm taking you home."

"But—"

"Forget it," he said tightly. Nodding to the security guard, he opened the door for Lynda and led her toward his car, already waiting at the curb. "I brought you here, and it's my responsibility to see you home safely." He pressed a tip in the valet's hand and helped Lynda into the car.

The ride to her house seemed to take hours; neither spoke on the way. They pulled into her driveway, and the car had barely stopped when Lynda was out and racing toward her door without a backward glance, fearing that at any minute Kent would stop her. He didn't.

Lynda slid the dead-bolt lock into place as soon as she closed the door. Leaning against it, she heard his car drive off, and tried to get her body to relax. She was home. She was safe. Just as he promised, a little voice deep inside her reminded.

I think you do need me. Kent's words sounded in her mind. For the rest of the night, she heard that statement and his declaration of love as clearly as if he'd been in the room with her. And just as clearly, the voice of her conscience screamed that she didn't need anyone. She was an adult now. That little girl who had trusted and loved had grown up. She was safe now, safer than she'd ever been in her life. And she didn't have to depend on anyone for that safety. She, alone, was in control of it. She alone, all alone.

"You look like something the cat dragged in," Suzanne stated with a concerned frown when Lynda stumbled into the kitchen late Saturday morning.

"I—I'm not feeling very well," Lynda said, hoping her family would assume she'd actually come down with some physical ailment. It was summer, and flu wasn't very likely, but her head was pounding and her body was so shaky, she felt as if she had a fever.

"Is that why you came home last night?" Suzanne asked, filling the teakettle. "Tea?"

"That sounds good," Lynda answered, ignoring the earlier statement.

"Here, Aunt Lyndy," Moe said softly, her little face concerned as she handed her aunt a battered stuffed animal. "Lambie will make you feel better."

With tears in her eyes, Lynda clutched her niece's favorite companion. Moe's offering her beloved stuffed lamb was her way of offering the ultimate consolation. "Thank you, baby," she said, and hugged her niece.

Moe's chubby little arms wrapped around Lynda, and she hugged her back. "I love you, Aunt Lyndy, and I want you to get better."

"Me too," Arrie added, and joined in the hugging.

Lynda doubted she'd ever feel better, but she couldn't tell them that. A shuddering sob escaped her throat, and her tears flowed freely down her cheeks as she held the two little girls. They were so trusting and so simplistic in their love. Lynda wished with all her heart that she could be like that again. She hugged them a little tighter, almost fearing that if she let go, she'd never be able to hold them again.

Suzanne sat down at the table and poured two cups of tea. "You want to talk about what's really wrong with you?"

"There's absolutely nothing wrong with me," Lynda snapped, then quickly apologized. Before she could say more, her tears started up again, and Suzanne was at her side in a flash and putting her arms around her sister. For the first time ever, it was the little sister consoling and protectively holding the big sister, and the turnaround was Lynda's undoing. Everything that had happened and had been said between her and Kent the night before tumbled out.

"You have been a good mother," Suzanne affirmed when Lynda had finished. "Except for one thing."

Sniffling into the tissue Suzanne handed her, Lynda asked, "What's that?"

"You're making me feel guilty about growing up and leaving you, and that's not fair."

"I object!" a deep male voice sounded from the back door. "All's fair in love and war."

"Kent!" At the sight of the raven-haired man entering the kitchen, Lynda felt her body warm. Gripping the edge of the table, she tried to shroud herself with the protective cover of anger, but it was difficult to keep from flinging herself into Kent's arms.

"Good to see you Kent. Sorry I can't stay longer, the girls and I are about to...eh...do the marketing," Suzanne said, ushering her daughters out of the house.

"Sorry you have to leave," Kent told her, keeping his gaze on Lynda. When they were alone, he said, "I did a lot of thinking last night after you left. I've figured you out, and you are really a fraud."

"You accused me of that before, and I'm going to give you the same answer as I did then. I am not a fraud!"

"Yes, you are."

Crossing her arms, Lynda huddled in her chair. The man was impossible. "There's no reasoning with you."

"I'm a reasonable man. It's you who can't reason."

Lynda let out a snort of derision.

"You look terrible," Kent said after a moment.

Lynda looked at him closely. His clothes were rumpled. His cheeks showed the stubble of a night's growth of beard. His eyes were bloodshot and underlined with dark shadows. Yet he was still the most handsome man she'd ever seen. "You look terrible, too."

"We're a perfect pair, then," he said, hunkering down in front of her. He smiled. "In fact, that's exactly what the problem is. I'm just too perfect for you, aren't I?"

Seething with exasperation, Lynda shook her head. "And just what does that mean?"

His expression stilled and grew serious. "That you're afraid I won't last. That I'll disappear suddenly."

Caught off guard, she was too surprised to do more than stare at him.

"Take a good look at me, Lynda," he directed. Straightening, he slowly turned in a complete circle. "Who do you see?"

"I see Kent Berringer, one of *the* Berringers," she mocked lightly. "Attorney and trombone player *extraordinaire*."

"And?" he prompted.

"And?" she echoed, confused and growing more and more annoyed. "Tall, dark and handsome with the most perfect body I've ever seen. Is that what your ego wanted to hear?"

He shook his head very slowly. "My ego has absolutely nothing to do with this. It's in splinters at your feet anyway, in case you really want to know where it is. Take a real good look and believe what you're seeing," he ordered. Bending down again, he brought his face within inches of hers. "Eyes are your business, Doctor. What exactly do you see here?"

Lynda didn't know what she was supposed to say and remained silent. "Don't be afraid," Kent said gently. "Take a real good look. I'm not going to disappear, I promise. You're looking at the man who loves you with all his heart and is asking you to trust his love and the love you have for him."

"But I don't—"

"Trust and honesty," Kent interrupted, not budging an inch away from her. "Now tell me exactly what you see."

His deep blue eyes were warm, honest and so compelling. Lynda couldn't mistake the message they were sending. "The man who loves me," she said softly.

"Very good. Your vision is perfect," he pronounced. Cradling her face between his palms, he gazed deeply into her eyes. "Am I seeing what I think I'm seeing, Doctor?"

If his ego was splintered at her feet, hers had joined the pile. He hadn't been quite correct in his assessment that he was too perfect for her. He was exactly perfect for her, and she wanted him so much it was frightening. A large lump formed in her throat, and she couldn't answer him.

Recognizing her fear for what it was, Kent prompted, "Trust me. Trust us. That's what love is really about. I do love you, Lynda. I'm promising to trust the rest of my life to you."

Lynda swallowed the lump in her throat, but she couldn't stop the tears that formed in her eyes. She wanted more than anything in the world to trust him. "I'm afraid," she whispered.

"I am, too," he said. "It's scary trusting someone, but it's even more scary not to trust. Then you're all alone in the world. That's not what you want, is it?"

Lynda shook her head. Though still a little bit afraid to reach out and take all that Kent Berringer was, she knew he was right. She was more afraid of not taking. She lifted one hand and curved it to his cheek.

Kent turned his face into her hand and kissed her palm. Smiling, he prompted again, "Now tell me what I'm seeing."

Swallowing her fears, Lynda dared to tease, "You do have a bit of a problem at near point, Mr. Berringer. I don't usually provide the answers for my patients, but you are a special case. What you're seeing is the woman who loves you."

"I'm not sure that's all the chart says," he remarked thoughtfully. "I think there's a bit more near the bottom, but you're going to have to tell me what it says. Maybe you'd better stand up, so I can get a better look."

"I believe you need further testing," she told him as she stood.

She leaned all her weight into his body. He didn't waver. This man wasn't going anywhere.

Feeling more courageous by the second, she laid her hands on his chest, felt the hard muscles that indicated his physical strength. Beneath those muscles lay his heart, beating steadily and dependably. *He* was dependable and would always be there. She said, "Now you should be able to read the bottom line."

Squinting, he murmured, "Mmm. I think it says she trusts me and believes in me."

"Very good," Lynda murmured in return, and rewarded him with a light kiss on his lips. "I believe you'll be needing to make an appointment for the rest."

"There's more?"

She nodded, smiling up at the man she was vowing to trust with the rest of her life. "I can work you in about a month from today, say about two-thirty in the afternoon?"

Gathering her closer, he lowered his head. Against her lips, he asked, "Too far away. I'm a desperate case."

"If you'd like a really long appointment—" she wound her arms around his neck and kissed him long and thoroughly "—one that starts with a small gathering at a beautiful old church on Cambridge Boulevard and continues for a week or two at some exotic place, you'll have to wait about a month."

"Doctor, I think I'm going to need an even longer appointment than that. Say, fifty years or so?"

"At the exotic place?"

"No, I guess the fifty years or so ought to be at a house with a big yard with a hedge, some kids and a dog. Can you work all that in?" he asked.

"Arrangements could be made for a special case like yours. Maybe we could discuss that somewhere." Pausing, she smiled seductively. "Somewhere more comfortable."

Kent raised an eyebrow in pretended skepticism. "You're not going to pretend that you don't want me to carry you into your bedroom, are you?"

"Why would I do a thing like that?" Lynda asked saucily. "That would certainly be perverse when we both know I find caveman tactics rather interesting."

"But I'm a Berringer, and we're a very dignified, respectable family," he maintained.

"What a fraud you are! You're the black sheep of the flock, and you'd better stay that way," she told him, and for insurance against further argument, she rose on her toes and covered his mouth with hers. Kent didn't protest. He gathered her up in his arms and she directed him to her bedroom.

They joined together in passion and tenderness. Each promised and trusted that their love was given and received in complete honesty. Lynda's last thought before Kent took her again was that this man, this perfect man, was hers forever and nothing would ever snatch him away.

It was a long time later when, nestled in each other's arms, sleep about to overtake them, Lynda asked, "Got any plans tomorrow?"

"Just spending it with you," Kent replied drowsily.

"Do you want the hedge or the lawn?"

Her question was answered with a groan. A nightmarish image of a future of miles and miles of overgrown hedges prompted Kent to comment, "On second thought, let's not have a hedge around that house we're going to live in for fifty years."

"Taking back a promise already?"

"You've got the hedge on one condition. We hire someone to trim it."

"But—"

"Shh, Ms. Do-it-all-herself, we can afford it. Trust me."

"I do."

* * * * *

COMING NEXT MONTH

#535 WILDERNESS CHILD—Ann Major
December's *Man of the Month*, Tad Jackson, wasn't about to be
burned twice by the woman who'd betrayed him—but the fire
between him and Jessica Bancroft Kent raged out of control.

#536 THE DIAMOND'S SPARKLE—Celeste Hamilton
Public relations man Nathan Hollister lived his life the same way
he drove his car . . . fast. Beautiful Liz Patterson could be the one
obstacle that slowed him down!

#537 HALFWAY TO HEAVEN—Katherine Granger
Lindsey Andrews wanted it all—the perfect career *and* the perfect
man. Jed Wentworth offered her both, but she couldn't mix
business with pleasure—could she?

#538 BEDSIDE MANNER—Jo Ann Algermissen
Though her job was at stake, Dr. Kristie Fairbanks was tempted
to give in to Joshua Hayden, the one man who could threaten her
career . . . and her heart.

#539 READ BETWEEN THE LINES—Erica Spindler
Sociology professor Katherine Reed needed a roommate for a
research experiment, and her old "friend" Michael Tardo kindly
volunteered. Unfortunately, he was still charming . . . and she was
still in love.

#540 CHRISTMAS STRANGER—Joan Hohl
It was a cold, snowy night when Virginia Greyson met Matthew
Hawk. He was the gift of a lifetime. But would fate take him as it
had so mysteriously brought him?

AVAILABLE NOW:

SILHOUETTE DESIRE™
presents
AUNT EUGENIA'S TREASURES
by CELESTE HAMILTON

Liz, Cassandra and Maggie are the honored recipients of Aunt Eugenia's heirloom jewels...but Eugenia knows the real prizes are the young women themselves. Every other month from December to April in Silhouette Desire, read about Aunt Eugenia's quest to find them worthy men and a treasure more valuable than diamonds, rubies or pearls—lasting love.

Coming in December: THE DIAMOND'S SPARKLE

Altruistic attorney Liz Patterson balks at Aunt Eugenia's attempt at matchmaking. Clearly, a shrewd PR man isn't her type. Nathan Hollister, after all, likes fast cars and fast times, but, as he tells Liz, love is something he's willing to take *very* slowly.

In February: RUBY FIRE

Passionate Cassandra Martin has always been driven by impulse. After traveling from city to city, seeking new opportunities, Cassandra returns home...ready to re-kindle the flame of young love with the man she never forgot, Daniel O'Grady.

In April: THE HIDDEN PEARL

Maggie O'Grady loved and lost early in life. Since then caution has been her guide. But when brazen Jonah Pendleton moves into the apartment next door, gentle Maggie comes out of her shell and glows in the precious warmth of love.

Aunt Eugenia's Treasures
Each book shines on its own, but together they're priceless

SD-AET-1

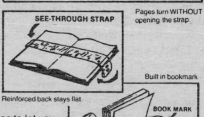

FOUR UNIQUE SERIES
FOR EVERY WOMAN YOU ARE...

Silhouette Romance

Love, at its most tender, provocative,
emotional...in stories that will make you laugh and
cry while bringing you the magic of falling in love.

6 titles per month

Silhouette Special Edition

Sophisticated, substantial and packed with
emotion, these powerful novels of life and love will
capture your imagination and steal your heart.

6 titles per month

Silhouette Desire

Open the door to romance and passion. Humorous,
emotional, compelling—yet always a believable
and sensuous story—Silhouette Desire never
fails to deliver on the promise of love.

6 titles per month

Silhouette Intimate Moments

Enter a world of excitement, of romance
heightened by suspense, adventure and the
passions every woman dreams of. Let us
sweep you away.

4 titles per month

SILG-1R

Wonderful, luxurious gifts can be yours with proofs-of-purchase from any specially marked "Indulge A Little" Harlequin or Silhouette book with the Offer Certificate properly completed, plus a check or money order (do not send cash) to cover postage and handling payable to Harlequin/Silhouette "Indulge A Little, Give A Lot" Offer. We will send you the specified gift.

Mail-in-Offer

OFFER CERTIFICATE

Item:	A. Collector's Doll	B. Soaps in a Basket	C. Potpourri Sachet	D. Scented Hangers
# of Proofs-of -Purchase	18	12	6	4
Postage & Handling	$3.25	$2.75	$2.25	$2.00
Check One				

Name _____

Address _____ Apt. # _____

City _____ State _____ Zip _____

ONE PROOF OF PURCHASE

To collect your free gift by mail you must include the necessary number of proofs-of-purchase plus postage and handling with offer certificate.

SD-2

Harlequin®/Silhouette®

Mail this certificate, designated number of proofs-of-purchase and check or money order for postage and handling to:

INDULGE A LITTLE
P.O. Box 9055
Buffalo, N.Y. 14269-9055